DEATH BY PREJUDICE

DEATH BY PREJUDICE

Jane McLoughlin

ROBERT HALE · LONDON

Typeset in 12/15 pt Sabon
by Derek Doyle & Associates, Shaw Heath.
Printed in Great Britain by
St Edmundsbury Press, Bury St Edmunds, Suffolk.
Bound by Woolnough Bookbinding Ltd.

what happened, I want everyone to understand that I wasn't the sort of person normally given to outlandish acts.

That night I could hear the rain hammering on the dark glass of the windows as I put on my coat. Nothing unusual about that. Castleborough was a city known for its cold wet winters and even wetter and only slightly less cold summers.

'It looks like you'll have a quiet night,' I said to Frank.

'That's all you know,' Frank said. He peered at me over the black plastic rims of his practically antique National Health glasses. 'You off?'

'I am.'

'See you in the pub later?' Frank asked.

'Not tonight,' I said.

'Not any night, these days,' he said. 'What's going on?'

'A secret lover, of course,' I said, and laughed.

'You're kidding.' Frank looked more gloomy than ever. 'No one could keep a lover secret in this place.'

'True enough. So maybe I've got something better to do than spend every night in the pub like the rest of you, OK?'

'Stop kidding yourself,' Frank said, and his voice left no room for doubt.

I didn't defend myself against Frank's prejudices because in some odd way I found them comforting. They were enduring and immutable, essentially English, like the rain, like the cliffs above Castleborough Sands, or the flow of the river under the ancient bridge in the city centre. Frank knew where he was in life and I knew where I was with Frank.

As usual when I didn't rise to his bait, he turned sulky. 'You're no different from the rest of us, you've nothing better to do with your money than piss it up the wall,' he said. The way he said 'pissing up the wall' made me one of the boys, and it actually pleased me. 'OK,' he said, 'you've got a mortgage, but you've no children to support. And no ex-wives.'

'I'd hardly have one of those,' I said.

'What? Oh, you know what I mean.' He sounded burdened, rather than bitter. Then he rallied and said, 'No, admit it, you must be writing a novel.'

'See you tomorrow, Frank.'

'Am I in it?' he asked. 'I've always wanted to be in one of those lurid sex sagas you women write. If you want to check my credentials any time, you've only to say.'

I let him have the last word.

I wished I could tell him the truth. I'd have liked to see his face if I turned up in the pub one night with Simon West. Frank was a professional cynic, but I knew he'd be impressed. His views on women were fixed back when females were either dependent wives or lesbians, meaning all the women who wouldn't come through for him of course. After his wife left him and took his kids with her, he'd even less time for the entire sex. But Frank did admire success wherever he saw it. If he saw me with Simon, he'd see Simon as a genuine trophy for me. Simon was a star. He was much more than a local television personality: he was a network celebrity. Simon West was, as Frank himself would've said, mega.

So I liked the idea of impressing Frank with my relationship with Simon. Frank thought I was one of those plain girls men don't bother with – anyway not until they were older and the hot numbers had burned their fingers. Actually, I often thought that way about myself, not exactly, as I've said, particularly plain, but certainly as the second-time-around type. I'd often wondered what Simon saw in me. I supposed I made him feel safe. He wasn't stupid; he knew the sort of bitches those good-looking girls around him were. I was different, and he liked that about me. This didn't always make me feel great, and I sometimes longed to be one of the hot numbers, but then we plain girls are always a bit vulnerable on the self-esteem front.

Anyway, I couldn't tell Frank. Simon and I'd agreed to

keep our relationship secret. Simon didn't have to tell me that his success depended on the adoration of millions of emotionally supercharged females. He traded on being the dream lover of pubescent young girls; of lonely females on the brink of middle age, and of still older women unwilling to accept that they were past romance. The sexual frisson of all those fantasies depended on his being unattached. I knew that as well as he did. An acknowledged live-in girlfriend would be a slap of reality across the face of the female fans' illusions, too real altogether. He couldn't risk it. He had to be seen to be available. Like it or not, I knew how much it all meant to him. If I'd spoiled it by making a fuss, I'd have lost him. And I loved him.

So we avoided being seen together in public. We never went out as a couple, or to meet friends. Actually, we were never even invited to meet friends. Simon didn't have friends. He had hangers-on, like publicity girls and personal trainers and secretaries. And my mates were the people at work, and I'd stopped socializing with them when I started seeing Simon. They were newspaper people and by definition that meant they couldn't keep a secret.

So Simon came to my house late at night. He had an apartment in a prestigious housing development in the old docks area. I'd never even seen inside it. Because of the sort of people who lived there, there was always the chance of a photographer lurking for a lucky break. I lived in a converted mews cottage tucked away behind a shopping street. I bought it because I could afford the mortgage, but it could've been designed as a secret hideout for illicit lovers. Even on late-night shopping days, everyone was gone before Simon came round, and he always went home before dawn, long before the vans started deliveries at the back entrances of the shops.

We spent nights and occasional weekends there together. Not often, though, because Simon was usually working, most often in London. The kind of game shows he presented and the live chat shows he appeared on as guest or host were strictly the stuff of weekend television.

I didn't mind. The lifestyle suited me. I liked being able to live my own life within our relationship. It wouldn't have been the same at all if people knew about us. I didn't want to lose my own identity to become a celebrity's girlfriend. I'd made a place for myself in Castleborough, which was another world after the chocolate-box West Country village where I'd grown up. I was proud of that. I liked the anonymity and the variety of a great provincial city; I felt at home there, secure in my pretty little house only a stone's throw from the great romantic river which had its source in the wild country towards the Border and flowed inexorably into the adventure of the sea.

The last thing I wanted was to be part of Simon's celebrity circus. I'd got my own career to establish. I saw myself one day editing a provincial daily newspaper just like the *Castleborough Gazette*. I wanted to win respect, not as a woman, but as a professional journalist. Being some sort of celebrity accessory wasn't the way to achieve that.

I'd no illusions about the vagaries of love, either. I would be twenty-six next birthday and, as Frank tended to say when I put off one of his clumsy late-night attempts to get me into bed, I'd been round the block a few times. I knew Simon was surrounded by available women more attractive than me. And, already, younger. It seemed to me that if I wanted a real future with Simon, I couldn't compete with these girls; I'd got to keep pace with him as a person in my own right. That was the only way I could see to offer him something different from the rest.

Of course with a good-looking man who spends a lot of time away from home surrounded by hot women, there's one thing a woman has to face and that's the jealousy issue. I

knew from the start Simon was bombarded by seductive little
sirens and dedicated trophy hunters. Frank might call it
whistling in the dark, but I thought there was safety in
numbers, other women were a fact of Simon's life, so the
more the merrier. I accepted that. His other women didn't
seem to have much to do with me.

That's what I told myself, anyway, and most of the time I
believed it. I'd almost got out of the habit of interrogating
him about who was with him whenever I telephoned him.

I loved Simon because he was sweet and kind and he made
me laugh. Of course I fancied him, too, but more than that
there was something vulnerable about him, a hint of past
suffering, that perhaps brought out my maternal instinct. I
told myself he needed me. Of course, I knew he didn't realize
it, but I knew he did and I loved him for it. I gave him an
emotional base, and that's why I trusted his love for me.

Who was I kidding? I loved Simon because I loved him.
There was nothing reasoned about it. When I wasn't with
him I thought about him. It seemed to me I was only alive
when we were together, and the rest of the time everything
was on hold. I didn't want it that way; I didn't like being in
thrall like that, even if no one except me knew about it, but
I was. I stopped nagging him about who he was with because
I knew I was driving him away and there was nothing I could
do about it if he wasn't alone.

I told myself, one day things would be different, what he'd
got right now wasn't going to last forever. One day, he'd lose
his looks; he'd be too old to hack it as a sex symbol. Then
there'd be me. How pathetic was that?

Simon knew that he couldn't be a sex symbol for ever. At
least his agent, Mal, was always telling him so. 'Make the
most of it while you can,' Mal said, 'nothing lasts in this
world.'

And yes, it did sometimes bother me that the great togeth-

11

erness that I craved depended on what would certainly be a crisis for Simon. But I told myself I'd deal with that when the time came. One day, not yet.

Now, as I left the newspaper office by the works entrance I was thinking only of whether Simon would come round later. I was feeling lonely.

The alley leading to the car park looked sinister in the lashing rain. The few street lights did their best but all that they illuminated was the blank reflection of wet black plastic rubbish bags long ignored by the municipal refuse collectors. Humanity seemed to have abandoned the place, and me with it.

I found myself wishing my life was more like that of some of the women in the office, doing the school run before work, racing out to shop at the supermarket on the way home to the family. At least those women knew where they belonged. Outside working hours, I was in limbo; waiting and waiting for nothing to happen.

Then I thought, to hell with it. I wanted to be somewhere warm and dry and full of ordinary people having a good time.

So I turned back the way I'd come, back along the side of the newspaper offices away from the car park and towards the teeming life of the city's main street. It didn't seem to matter to the people there that it was raining. They seemed able to ignore the weather. The shops and street lighting glared like the midnight sun. People in the street were too busy to notice the cold and wet. They were too involved in living their lives to notice.

The newspaper's local, The Turk's Head, was crowded with reporters and sub-editors. Most of the reporters who'd come off the day shift were still there. And several men on the late shift were taking an early break. On the widescreen television above the bar, Simon, looking rather orange, was hosting a quiz show. It was very popular, on at a peak time, but it wasn't my kind of thing. I'd told Simon that. He just laughed. But it felt odd having him there in the pub with people who'd no idea that he and I were an item.

Pete, the barman, poured me a dry white wine without being asked. 'Long time no see,' he said. 'It's gone up tuppence since you were last here.'

Nothing else had changed. Same old faces, same old talk of intros and bylines and brilliant headlines; same old gossip.

I'd almost forgotten that this was where I really felt at home. I wondered what it must be like to be married to one of these newspaper men? They probably spent as little time at home with their families as Simon did with me. But at least their partners didn't have to worry about them having it off with someone else: reporters were reporters, amongst themselves they were all sexless the moment they came into the pub. It was usually the stay-at-home spouses who found someone else. Frank wasn't the only one it had happened to.

I took my drink and joined a group further up the bar.

The late-shift reporter, Ted Ellis, was already drunk. He had the face of a two-legged pig with his turned-up snout and little light-lashed eyes. But there was something more dangerous about him than that, the pitiless expression of a wild boar lurked behind those pale eyes.

'Frank been in?' I asked.

His plump pink face looked blank for a moment, as though he'd never heard of Frank. Then he said, 'Frank? Must've been a hold up. He'll be along.'

And then the mobile phone beside his tankard on the bar rang.

'Right on cue,' he said, 'yes, Frank?'

His face changed as he listened. I'd seen this before so often I almost laughed, the boozy slob suddenly transformed as his brain locked on to a story.

13

'What is it this time?' I asked him, when he put the phone down. 'Another of our MP's love-kids turned up?'

Ted, self-important, drained the last of his pint. 'Better than that,' he said. 'This one will make the lead in the nationals tomorrow.' He wiped his mouth with his sleeve.

'Well?'

'It's Simon West,' he said.

A cold fist of fear thumped me in the gut. The bar seemed to tilt and the wine in my glass sloshed over and ran down the front of my jeans.

'What's happened?' I said. It was amazing Ted didn't notice how strange my voice sounded.

On the television screen, Simon was laughing.

'God's gift to Britain's female population has been arrested,' Ted said.

He didn't try to conceal the note of gloating. He paused, timing his announcement like a stand-up comedian.

'He's been arrested. Simon West has been arrested for rape!'

2

'Bastards, you know it isn't true'

I was scarcely aware of what I was doing after that.

I followed Ted out into the rain-swept street and then into the foyer of the newspaper. But when he got into the lift to go up to the newsroom, I turned and ran back out into the street.

I couldn't go into the office. My shift was over, I had no point there. I could think of only one place to go. I went home.

I wasn't aware of driving through the city centre traffic to my own quiet backwater, nor of parking the car. I wasn't aware of the rain pouring down my face and neck, or my bedraggled hair and soaked clothes. I opened my front door like a zombie, walked into the sitting-room, and closed the curtains. Then I turned on the light.

The silence in the house seemed like a threat. I put my hands over my ears and pressed to shut out that ominous quiet. My brain felt as though it was about to pop.

I repeated Ted's words aloud: 'Simon West has been arrested for rape.'

I sat on the sofa and stared at the empty grate. Less than

twenty-four hours ago Simon and I had sat together and stared at the flames. And now this.

I was more bewildered than angry at first. It wasn't true. How could anyone think Simon was a rapist? It wasn't possible.

'It's not even logical,' I said aloud. 'Why would someone like Simon rape anyone? It isn't as though he can't have any girl he wants. He'd never need to rape anyone.'

I heard Frank's voice echo in my head, 'You're whistling in the dark.'

Rape wasn't about sex, I knew that, every woman knew that. Rape was about power.

And that was just as ridiculous, of course. Simon wasn't some sort of pathetic inadequate.

But all the same a prosecuting-counsel doubt gnawed at the back of my mind. How well did I really know Simon, really know him? Our relationship was clandestine, it wasn't normal. I didn't know anything about what Frank would call 'his roots'. He'd never talked about his childhood. Perhaps he hated women because he wanted to get even with his mother, or his sisters bullied him.

I'd assumed his parents were dead. He'd never mentioned them. I didn't know if he had sisters, or brothers, come to that. He'd have told me if he'd got siblings. Wouldn't he? I couldn't not be aware of something like that.

Maybe it was odd that he'd never mentioned his family, but I'd never told him anything about mine, either. I'd deliberately cut myself off from my past, too. I'd no control over that, I could create the present for myself. Why shouldn't he, too? There'd been magazine profiles; he told the interviewers whatever he thought they wanted to hear. He and I used to laugh about the lurid tales he got away with. As far as I was concerned, he'd sprung to fame from nowhere and no one, and that was fine by me. He'd never shown the slightest interest in my life before we met, so why should I in his?

I assumed he was like me. I'd had a strong need to deny – no, deny was too strong a word – to obscure my conventional background. I wanted to retain some mystery about myself. I was only too well aware how women like me are typecast.

I never really succeeded in reinventing myself like Simon did, though; he really was whatever anyone wanted him to be. If he'd wanted to talk about all that, he would've done.

But now I couldn't stifle that hateful, treacherous whisper in my head. Why was I thinking like this? And why should a woman make accusations if there was nothing in it?

Because she was a bitch, of course, a manipulating bitch. Or there'd been some stupid mistake, that was what'd happened. It needed sorting, that was all.

I made an effort to pull myself together. I even tried to laugh at myself. What kind of a journalist did I think I was, giving credence to such sensational nonsense? Of course it wasn't true. It was just some silly rumour that came into the office and of course Frank had to get a reporter to check it.

That happened all the time on newspapers, and the stories were hardly ever true when they were checked out.

I was an idiot, jumping to conclusions like that. It wasn't professional.

I'd done such a good job of convincing myself I turned on the television for the News.

There was a picture of Simon amongst a group of thuggy men. He looked shocked. His face was drawn and he hadn't shaved. It was the lead story.

Television Star Accused of Rape. Simon West Arrested.

I clutched my mouth and raced for the lavatory. I only just made it before I threw up.

By the time I'd stopped retching, the news was almost

over. The presenter repeated the summary: 'The television celebrity Simon West has been accused of rape. Police have arrested the star and are holding him in custody.'

Signed, sealed, and delivered, the words pounded through my head.

'Bastards, you know it isn't true,' I screamed at the newsreader. And at the police, and at the reporters rattling out their stories for tomorrow's papers.

They always had it in for people like Simon. They were always jealous of success. Repeating what they'd been told, like parrots, without a thought for what they were saying, without even questioning whether it was likely that someone like Simon West would have to rape any woman he wanted. No one even acknowledged the possibility that it was just the sort of thing some demented bitch would make up. To get revenge for some imagined rejection. Or just to draw attention to herself.

I was shocked at the sound of my own voice screeching.

Stop it, I told myself, you've got to stay in control. You've got to think clearly. Simon needs you to do that.

Surely the police couldn't arrest somebody just like that, without evidence? But they did, all the time. And of course, arrest didn't mean charged, it just meant someone was being questioned. They used to say 'helping the police with their inquiries' but that had come to have an old-fashioned ring of possible innocence, so they started saying arrested because it made people think they were getting somewhere when they weren't.

Did I really believe that? Even if the newspapers and television reporters might seem to take up anyone's story to discredit a celebrity, surely the police wouldn't? They must think they'd got some sort of case. But the police had an axe to grind. They were more interested in covering their backs than in justice. According to the court reports, they made up evidence all the time to fit people up.

I found I could scarcely move; all my joints seemed to hurt, as though I'd been given a kicking. My eyes hurt, too.

My hands were shaking as I poured myself a drink. I chipped the glass against the rim of the bottle as I poured, so I swigged from the bottle. I could scarcely swallow, though, my throat seemed to be blocked. Whisky bubbled out of my mouth and ran down my chin.

I was very cold. My clothes were still drenched from the rain, but I couldn't summon the energy to change. I sat stiffly on the sofa and stared at the silent telephone.

Thank God no one knew about Simon and me, they'd all be on the phone wanting to talk about it. That would've been horrible. But then, sitting beside the telephone staring at the dead fire, I felt bereft at the lack of anyone to talk to. Even Frank would've been better than no one. There was no one in the world I could tell now. I'd spent too many Christmases alone, thinking how everyone else was loved and needed enough to have somewhere to go, to know what it felt like to be lonely, but this was something else.

As the hours passed, my feet and fingers grew numb. When at last the telephone rang I could scarcely pick it up to answer it.

'Sara?' Simon's voice sounded thin, as though it was painful for him to speak.

'You've heard?' he said.

'Simon, what's happening? Where are you?' I tried to stem the flood of questions I had to ask.

'I'm at Mal's.'

I felt a moment's wild joy. They'd let him go. Then indignation followed the happiness, that the police could have put him through this knowing they'd never really had a case; I hoped he'd make them pay, he couldn't ignore such malice.

Then came doubt. He didn't sound like a free man.

'Did they drop the charges?'

'No, Mal came up with the bail. They let him take me home.'

I knew then what people meant when they said their blood ran cold with fear.

And why Mal? Why did he turn to Mal, not me?

I hated myself for thinking like this. Of course Mal was the person he'd turn to. Mal was his spokesman. And also some sort of father figure. Mal also controlled Simon's money.

And I understood why Simon hadn't involved me. It was for my own sake.

But surely he couldn't shut me out now? I didn't know what I was thinking of, I should have gone straight down to the police station to support him. I'd let him down.

At the same time I couldn't help a niggling feeling that he'd made it impossible for me to go to him, and that somehow that was disloyal of him. How could I think like that? But I did, and hated myself for it.

He said, 'Oh, my God, Sara, what's happening?'

I could hear the fear in his voice and I suddenly realized the enormity of what he faced. I tried to sound confident.

'Simon, you've got to keep calm. It's all some hideous mistake, it must be. We'll sort it out. Do you know who's doing this to you, the woman who accused you? Have you seen a lawyer?'

He seemed to be fighting for breath on the line, then Mal's big fruity voice boomed in my ear:

'Is this Sara? Hello. I'm Mal, our boy's agent. You're not to worry, you hear? I'm sure this can be sorted out, but for now I've got Simon out on bail as long as he stays here with me. He'll have to appear in court in the next few days, and then perhaps we'll find out what this is all about.'

'What's your address?' I said. 'I'll come down.'

Mal sounded embarrassed. 'I don't think that's such a

good idea,' he said. 'Simon's adamant you must be kept out of this. Maybe he'll think differently tomorrow; I'm sure maybe he will.'

'But I love him,' I said, not feeling the embarrassment I'd normally feel saying such a thing to a stranger. 'He needs me,' I added, and it sounded feeble even to me.

'I'm sorry, love, really I am, but I'm thinking of Simon. He's had a few drinks and taken a sedative and what he really needs now is rest. Now's not the time for emotional scenes, believe me. Maybe tomorrow.'

'But who's accusing him of rape? Who would do such a thing?'

Mal hesitated. It was as though I could hear his mind working as he tried to find the right words. 'I don't know,' he said. 'The police are playing this close to their chests and they're not saying anything at all to me. I suppose they're afraid we'd try to get at her if we knew who she was.'

'But what are they accusing him of? Rape covers anything from trying to force the pace on a date to leaping out of the bushes and forcing yourself on a stranger. What are the circumstances of the charge?'

I heard myself sounding as though I was interviewing the chief constable.

'It's not at all clear yet,' Mal said. He sounded weary. 'Putting two and two together, I think the allegations are about incidents of date rape on the same woman about seven years ago. Honest, that's all I can say.'

'Doesn't anyone wonder why this alleged victim kept coming back for more?'

I knew I sounded unforgivably flippant, but in an effort to stay calm I was trying to respond like a reporter, clinically. I was afraid to show any emotion, because I was terrified I'd fall apart.

Mal was saying something. 'Look, love, you could do

something very important. Try to get Simon to see a solicitor, will you? The one thing he needs now is a lawyer, but he doesn't want a lawyer.'

'Of course he's got to get a solicitor. Why won't he?'

'He says if he does, it shows he accepts there's a case to answer. Which he insists there isn't. He thinks the police are out to get him. I think he hopes that when they see the newspapers, they won't want to risk the publicity when they have to backtrack. So he thinks the whole thing will disappear.'

I felt sorry for Mal then. I knew what Simon was like in that mood. In some ways all the fame and adulation had stopped him growing up, and when he most needed to be adult, he didn't know how and behaved like a small stubborn boy digging in his heels.

'Of course he's got to get a lawyer,' I said again. 'Tell him he'll need one to sue the police for damages. And this woman, whoever she is.'

'Will do,' Mal said. He hesitated, then added, 'He says to tell you he'll ring tomorrow. Don't worry, love, I'm sure this can be sorted. I'm sorry we had to meet this way . . .' He'd forgotten my name but he quickly added 'love' to cover himself. Then he laughed and said, 'I've heard a lot about you tonight considering I never knew you existed.'

I knew that this was the closest I was going to get to Simon for now. I was glad that Mal now knew about us, Simon and me. It was a kind of confirmation of our relationship.

'I'm sorry too about us meeting like this,' I said. 'He talks a lot about you. I'm glad he's got you now. Us, I mean. I'm glad he's got us.'

'I think he's going to need us both,' Mal said.

3

No Smoke Without Fire

Simon's first court appearance was a formality. Reporting restrictions wouldn't be lifted. We talked every day on the phone, always the kind of stilted, useless conversations spies in bad movies have on railway stations. Simon wouldn't let me see him at Mal's, the media had the place staked out. The court proceedings were my first chance to see him or speak to him face to face. I was actually looking forward to it as a chance of showing him I loved him and was there for him whatever happened.

But the night before he rang and asked me not to go.

'It'll be worse if you do,' he said. 'We both know only too well that once they know about you, those thwarted hacks would leap at the chance to make you into the story. Can't you see the headlines? ' *"I'll stand by my man', says disgraced star Simon's girl".'*

'But I want to stand by you. Wouldn't it help? I can tell them you're the last person in the world who'd ever rape anyone.'

'That's what they always say, the women behind the accused man.' Simon's attempt at a bitter laugh made my mouth go dry with fear. He seemed so distant, a stranger putting on a good show in public.

I could look after myself, he didn't have to protect me, but how could I tell him that? I understood that he needed to feel he was taking care of me. No, I didn't understand, but I tried to.

'I love you,' I said.

I wasn't sure we hadn't been cut off. He didn't say anything. 'I wish I could see you,' I said. It was like trying to get through to someone in a coma. 'It's hopeless trying to talk to you over the phone,' I said. There was so much I wanted to say and couldn't. 'I love you, Simon, and I miss you so much.'

Then he said, 'Please, Sara, don't get involved. I love you, too, and I don't want to let you be part of this. If you really love me, you'll understand.'

I knew what he was afraid of. I knew only too well that however staunchly I refused to answer the reporters' questions, they'd still make up their stories: *Rape Victim Lying for Money, says Simon's Sad Lover.*

So I didn't go to court. Instead I went to The Turk's Head well before I was due at work for the afternoon shift. I thought I could wait there without attracting attention until Ted came in for his usual liquid lunch. I'd checked the news list and I knew he was down to cover the restricted hearing.

When I got to the pub, the first thing I saw was Ted's piggy face soaking up the drink with a group from the newsroom. I joined them at the bar. Ted looked more porcine than usual with his bright little piggy, pink-rimmed, light-lashed eyes, but those eyes didn't miss much.

Before long someone asked, 'Anything come out of the Simon West business, Ted?'

Ted drained his pint and wiped his wet red lips on his sleeve. He was puffed up with his own importance, the possessor of secrets he could tell but wouldn't.

'You know the form,' he said, and shrugged. He imitated the flat monotone of a stonewalling official spokesman. 'The police are investigating,' he said, 'and in the light of evidence disclosed by their investigation, they have yet to decide if there's a case to answer.'

'So it's wait and see?'

'So they've renewed bail?'

'Care and control of his manager.'

Ted wasn't really interested. There wouldn't be a byline for him in this story until it came to trial. Women reporters were covering the colour stuff about betrayed fans, and broken dreams. The features department would be working on psychological analysis of the perils of celebrity.

'Have you any idea who's making the allegations?' My voice sounded unnaturally loud as I asked the question, but no one else seemed to notice.

Ted winked. 'Officially the police are keeping it to themselves at this stage,' he said. 'They say they're still making inquiries. But unofficially . . .' Ted couldn't resist being 'the man in the know'.

I wanted to slap his glistening pink pig's face.

'Come on, Ted, you must have some idea,' someone said.

Ted shook his head, putting his empty glass ostentatiously on the bar. 'No, no can do. A good mate on the police team told me in strictest confidence—'

The barmaid suddenly broke into the conversation. 'Simon West may be big here,' she said, 'but he doesn't compare with that singer he lived with who went to Hollywood. She's mega.' She cleared Ted's empty glass from the bar. 'She married a video producer and never looked back,' she added.

One of the reporters laughed. 'Marta Blane? So she did, I'd forgotten,' he said. 'Simon West threw her out because she was always on at him to marry her. She wouldn't leave him

25

alone. He had to ask for police protection.'

Ted didn't like the way attention had shifted from him. 'That's not quite right,' he said. 'He got an injunction. She was supposed to stay more than fifty metres away from him, but she kept breaking it. That's why the police were involved.' Ted liked to be exact.

'Well, one thing,' the barmaid said, 'Marta Blane's too big these days to bother accusing Simon West of rape.'

'She's not as big as she was; she could be trying to revive her career accusing West of rape. Wouldn't that be a story?' one of the reporters said, and everyone laughed except Ted.

He was sulking. 'Wouldn't she want it publicized if that were the case?' he said with heavy sarcasm. He moved to stand apart at the bar, looking superior.

I wanted to hear more about Simon and Marta Blane, but, pretending indifference, I went to stand close to Ted.

'You don't really know who this alleged victim is, do you, Ted?' I said. 'Bet you don't know anything at all, really, do you?'

'Bet I do,' Ted said.

'So prove it. Or admit it, you don't know any more than we do.'

Ted's professional pride was at stake. 'Of course I know. It's a woman called Midgley. So bollocks to you.'

'So who is she?'

'I don't know more than that.'

Ted obviously wished he hadn't said anything. He never felt at ease with me. He didn't like my university degree. He was always telling people how he was a graduate of the University of Life, unlike some – and then he'd look at me as though I was someone with learning difficulties, or a foreigner from some country where they don't play football. It was true my idea of sport was cricket or horse racing, and I couldn't even name most of the Castleborough United football team, even when they were close behind the leaders in the Premier League. I knew he didn't like me and never would, but this was the first time I wished he did.

'That's all I know,' he said. 'Except of course there's been a queue of little tarts outside the police station since he was arrested saying he did it to them, too.'

A sour-faced blonde called Petra who edited the women's page heard this as she joined the group. 'Well,' she said, 'he probably did screw them. The question is, was it rape? Or, more to the point, what exactly *is* rape?'

I had to bite my lower lip to stop myself attacking her. I couldn't very well tell her she didn't know what she was talking about.

'What do you think?' Ted asked her.

'Oh, of course I think he's guilty as hell,' said Petra. 'It's more than my life's worth to think a woman would lie about a thing like that. And, anyway,' she added, 'there's no smoke without fire, is there?'

I knew I was going to hear that expression again and again in the coming weeks. I couldn't bear to hear any more of her talk.

I walked out of The Turk's Head into the gloomy northern afternoon. I felt horribly alone. For the first time in my life, the future seemed full of menace, and I didn't like the feeling that there wasn't any reason to hope for things to get better.

An east wind funnelling between the office buildings cut like a knife as I made my way up the alley. I pulled my coat close and hurried towards the office.

Midgley, Midgley, Midgley, the name of Simon's accuser banged inside my head, swinging like a pendulum. I imagined her gloating as she watched the news bulletins on TV. Why had she done it? Was she sick in the head? I didn't feel sorry for her, I hated her, I wanted to kill her. But no, I told myself, if she died now, she'd never be proved a liar. She couldn't die yet, but one day. . . .

Oh God, Simon, I said to myself, what's going to happen to you?

And to us?

4

When the Kissing Stopped

The night after Simon's preliminary court appearance was a low point for me. That was the night I saw the future and didn't want to live through it. I tried reading, watching television, playing about on the Internet, but I couldn't put the Midgley woman and her rape charge out of my mind. I didn't exactly think that Simon might possibly *be* guilty, but I did think he could easily be found guilty and spend years in jail. What would happen to him was beyond imagining.

I was also thinking of myself.

Everything seemed pointless, and as though it always would. It wasn't the big things so much, it was the ordinary little things which no longer held any pleasure for me. I felt as though the light had gone out in my life and I dreaded living on and on in the dark. I tried not to think that if Simon had been killed in a car crash, at least I'd know that some time in the future I could move on. But the way things were going he'd be in jail, and then when he emerged he'd be ruined, and my love for him would be a cage I could never escape from. So would his need of me.

Of course I didn't like myself for thinking that way, but

however hard I tried not to, I couldn't help it.

I was finally on my way to bed when I heard a muffled sound from my small back garden. For a moment, I actually hoped someone had come to murder me.

Then came a tapping on the half-glazed kitchen door.

I could see the outline of a man in a jogger's anorak with a hood pulled up over his head. I opened the door and even as I did it, I knew how stupid I was being. It could be anyone.

So when I saw Simon, my annoyance with myself made me irritable with him.

'What's all the undercover stuff?' I demanded. 'You've got a key to the front door.'

'They're after me,' he said.

Did he mean the police, or the paparazzi? Instinctively I looked round to make sure he was alone.

'How'd you escape them?' I asked.

'Are you going to let me in?' he said, trying to push past me. 'They can't be far behind.'

I stood aside to let him in, then closed the door.

Simon was breathing hard. I could tell he'd been drinking. Well, so would I drink, in his situation.

'Those newspaper ghouls won't find me now,' he said. 'Mal and I were in his car and he did a few sneaky turns and let me out before leading them off somewhere at a rate of knots. He'll keep them at bay for a while, and even when they realize they've been fooled, he won't give anything away. I thought you'd let me hide out here.'

I was so glad to see him again, I wasn't going to argue. If he was breaking bail conditions or some official regulations, I didn't care.

'Of course you'll stay here,' I said. 'They've no idea where to look, and if you keep indoors, no one's likely to see you.'

I went to kiss him, but, laughing, he held me at arm's length.

'Let me get my breath,' he said. 'I'm covered in sweat.'

He shivered. 'It's freezing in here.'

It was as though we spoke different languages and were trying to communicate in one which neither of us had used outside the classroom.

'Come upstairs,' I said, 'the bed's warm.'

I longed for him to make love to me, even just hug me, anything to show that in spite of everything we were together. It wasn't just for me, I thought it would be what he wanted too.

'I'd rather have a drink,' he said.

I tried not to mind; he didn't mean me to take it literally; he probably was thirsty after running away from the photographers.

He went to the fridge and took out a bottle of vodka. 'You want one?'

It was weird, this unfamiliar stranger in my house behaving as though he was my Simon.

'Not now,' I said, 'it's a bit late for me.' It was the best I could do to make a feeble joke, but I couldn't help feeling some resentment at the way he was making himself at home. He seemed to me to be forcing me into the role of a sister, an older sister comforting a little brother frightened of the dark. But that wasn't how things were. I wanted him to comfort me, too. Stop it, I told myself, stop being daft.

I was being unreasonable because I wanted him to be pleased to be with me at last, but of course it wasn't like that for him. I knew that for him the last few days hadn't been about missing me, he'd had too much to occupy him for that. He was the one who was really suffering. After what he'd been through, I'd have wanted to drown my sorrows, too. But if I could see that about him, why couldn't he try to think what it was like for me? How could he? I couldn't blame him because I expected the impossible.

'OK, I'll join you for a quick one,' I said. Time enough for sorting things out once everything was a bit more normal.

But normality was a long way off. And in the circumstances, how could we possibly be normal around each other?

For the next few days, Simon stayed in the house and kept out of sight, but he wasn't the Simon I'd known. Mostly he stayed in bed late and then lay around in the sitting-room half the night without bothering to get dressed, waiting for me to come home from my shift and cook him something to eat. I found myself treating him as an invalid, and that was what he seemed to expect. He took it for granted, and his complacency made me want to scream.

I kept telling myself I must humour him because his entire world was collapsing around him. I did feel desperately sorry for him. But at the same time I couldn't help the niggling thought that he couldn't go on like this. I couldn't put things right alone, and he'd got to find a way to deal with it and survive.

But a treacherous little voice in my head said, Simon's not up to survival, he can't do anything to help himself. But if so, what was I supposed to do to help?

'You could make yourself a sandwich, Simon,' I said. 'You don't have to wait for me to come home to eat.'

'Someone might see me at the window,' he said. 'Best not to take risks.'

'Someone thinks you're using me,' I muttered, but when he asked what I'd said, I didn't repeat it.

He sat for hours during the day in the sitting-room with the blinds closed drinking vodka. By the time I got home he was drunk and often maudlin and I had to go out and get another bottle for him, but I didn't like to make a fuss about that, either.

At night, he paced my bedroom until I wanted to scream at him to give me a break, to sit still and let me sleep. I

32

wanted to tell him to stop guzzling the vodka and get a grip, but I said nothing. I was afraid he'd get angry and shout at me, or break down in tears. I wasn't sure which I'd find hardest to take, to be honest. Anyway, I always felt on the verge of tears myself.

Soon I began to dread coming home from work, knowing how he'd still be full of self-pity, obsessed by the unfairness of what the world was doing to him. At the same time, I knew he had every right to feel like that; he was going through hell. But I couldn't stop the way I kept thinking nasty thoughts about him because he wasn't helping himself. I looked at him sprawled on the sofa. Must he be so crushed? When was he going to start fighting back? And it never seemed to occur to him that all this business, with him hiding out in my house, was hard on me, too.

One evening I smelled burning as I came through the front door. I ran into the sitting-room where he was slumped on the leather sofa, glass in hand. The air was thick with cigarette smoke. He'd taken up smoking again since he'd been living with me.

'What's burning?' I shouted at him. 'Can't you smell something's on fire?'

He waved his glass at me.

He'd put down a lighted cigarette on the arm of the sofa and there was a smouldering hole in the leather.

I lost my temper.

'This is fucking awful!' I screamed. 'You've got to . . .'

But I couldn't say it, I was afraid to say he had to stop drinking.

'I've got to what?' he said.

'Oh, nothing,' I said. I looked at him slumped on my ruined sofa and I could scarcely stop myself attacking him, driving my fists through the stupid vacant expression on his handsome face.

I went to bed and cried myself to sleep.

This wasn't the way lovers were with one another. If only he'd say, just once, that he loved me, it would make everything all right. Of course none of this was his fault. He'd every reason to be the way he was. If only it didn't make me want to hit out and break down his listlessness.

Every day I had all the papers delivered. It was part of my job to read them before I went to work. Simon had got in the habit, as soon as he heard the letter box rattle in the morning, of rushing downstairs and bringing them upstairs to read in bed.

The morning after I'd chickened out of attacking him, he threw the tabloid he was reading across the room.

'Look at this,' he said. 'Another anonymous allegation against the villainous me.'

His flippant tone suggested he was actually making a joke of it, that was a good thing, surely?

'What did you do this time?' I tried to follow his lead and make light of it.

'Our wicked pervert made this girl's little sister watch while he subjected her to unspeakable abuse, and then committed perverted sexual practices on the child. I wonder what exactly those are?'

'Reading her extracts from *Grimm's Fairy Tales*, I expect,' I said.

But I wanted to weep for him, this was dreadful. How could he ever survive this kind of abuse?

'Sara, who *are* these women?' he said. 'What have I done to them?' His voice broke.

'The case is *sub judice*. They can't keep this up.'

'Not much sign of them dropping it. Even the *Guardian*'s got some pundit to speculate on why celebrities are more prone to sexual perversion than anyone else.'

'Why's that, then?'

'Because they get so much of the normal stuff they can't get it up without extra thrills, apparently. Or, on the other hand, they're so in love with themselves they think they've a divine right to use anyone they can get exactly as they please.'

'It makes a change from all those rent-a-mouth commentators going on about why women find famous men irresistible.'

Simon threw the rest of the papers to the end of the bed. 'You see, it's hopeless. They blame me anyway. It's not a question of guilty or innocent. That doesn't matter. The point is, I'm to blame.'

I pulled him down to kiss him.

He started to kiss me in return, but then he moved away abruptly.

'It's no good, I can't,' he said. 'If this nightmare goes on much longer, I'm done for.'

I tried to think of something to say to comfort him.

'Once you're proved innocent, you can sue everyone for damages,' I said. 'Then you'll be the good guy and everything will be OK again.'

I knew how feeble it sounded as I said it. If I'd been him, this kind of manic looking on the bright side would drive me mad. But what else could I say? Was this how all our future conversations would go – me pretending to optimism I didn't feel to cheer him up; him driven to greater gloom by the transparency of my pretence?

We were trying to protect each other, but we'd never be able to be honest with one another about this.

Simon said, '*If* I'm proved innocent. How can I prove I'm innocent when these women tell such lies? I'm supposed to be innocent till they prove I'm guilty. Fat chance of that.'

What was I supposed to say? Something fatuous like 'the truth will out'? I didn't believe that. I'd never been stupid enough to believe that. It was always the lies people believed.

I put my arms round him. 'Don't think about it,' I said, trying to kiss him, 'we've better things to do in bed.'

Simon turned his face to avoid my mouth. He pushed me away gently.

'Sorry, Sara, but not now.'

He got up and went to the bathroom.

I heard him bolt the door.

5

A Declaration of War

The next day I got to work early. Everyone was at lunch. A phone was ringing on the empty sub-editors' table. I picked it up.

I hadn't spoken to Simon's agent Mal since our telephone introduction on the night of Simon's arrest, but I recognized his booming voice at once. I was suddenly frightened.

'What is it?' I asked. 'What's happened?'

Mal sounded embarrassed. 'I thought I'd better warn you, love,' he said. 'Simon's lost his job. We'd been discussing his contract with the TV company before all this happened. I'd expected to get him a lot better deal this time, and now they've decided not to renew. They've put him on suspension in the meantime.'

I felt as though someone had hit me in the stomach.

'But they can't do that. It looks as though they think he's guilty. He hasn't been found guilty.'

The boom in Mal's voice sounded like an echo in empty space. 'I'm not going to let them off the hook, love, but I don't see there's much I can do. He is *Where There's Muck There's Brass.*' That was the name of Simon's current hit TV show. 'It's a prime-time family programme,' Mal said, 'and they don't think Simon's image is right any more. I'll get him a few thousand in lieu of notice, perhaps, but there wasn't much time to run on the old contract. There won't be much of a pay off.'

This was awful. It was bad enough waiting to hear if the police were going to trial, but to go through that without work to keep him occupied ... Simon couldn't deal with that.

I could hear the panic in my voice. 'Mal, for God's sake, they can't stop him working. How can they do this? He's the most popular star on television.'

'He *was* the most popular star,' Mal said. The boom in his voice was now a knell.

'Have you told Simon?' I asked. I was suddenly afraid he'd rung to ask me to do that. But I underestimated Mal.

'Yes,' he said, 'I told him. He's very upset. I wanted to warn you.' Even Mal was crying off.

I suddenly saw what was happening through Simon's eyes, and I quailed at the vision. No work to go to; no one to seek him out; nothing to do, and no one to turn to. Except me. I was there for him and I knew I wasn't enough.

'Mal,' I said, 'isn't there anything you can do? Simon can't live without work. He hasn't got anything else.'

'I'm doing my best. If the police don't go to trial, things may pick up. And he's got you. I told him, he's lucky to have you.'

'Yes, he's got me.' I felt sick. At that moment I'd willingly have killed the woman who started all this, the lying, sick, vicious bitch who'd accused him.

'Hang in there, love,' Mal said. 'While there's life and all that ...'

He could have been talking about a dead man.

I was like a robot all day at work. All I could think about

was getting home to Simon. I tried telephoning the house, but there was no reply. The unrequited ringing was frightening.

When my shift ended, though, I lingered in the office. I didn't want to go home. How could I comfort him when I'd nothing left to give?

When I did get there, Simon was sitting with the curtains drawn watching a children's video. He had finished one bottle of vodka and opened another.

The moment I came in the door, he came to me; he was like a small, sad child coming to its mother. I held him. We stood there together for a long time, clinging to each other.

'Oh, Sara,' he whispered, 'I can't tell you how good it is to see you.'

I couldn't speak. I nodded at him, tears burning my eyes.

He made a ghastly attempt to joke. 'I'll be seeing a lot more of you from now on, I expect,' he said. 'It seems not everyone wants to share their fireside telly of an evening with a known rapist.' He threw himself on to the sofa and pulled me down beside him. 'Sara, you do still believe I didn't do it, don't you?'

I put my fingers on his lips to stop him speaking.

At the same time I thought I should ask him who this Midgley woman was?

Several times before I'd tried to form the words, but then put it off. Deep down, I was afraid of what I might discover. And he might think I didn't trust him if he knew I'd been checking up on his case.

I shook my head, trying to smile at him. 'I know you didn't do it. And after the trial, if they even go ahead with one, everyone in the world will know you didn't. They'll have to admit they got it wrong. It's getting through the time till then that's going to be tough. But we've got each other.'

'They've got to go ahead with the trial now. I need them

to. If the police simply drop it, everyone's going to think there's some sort of conspiracy to protect me, or I bought off the woman. It's got to come to court.'

He touched my cheek. For a few minutes we sat together, hands clasped so tightly that our knuckles were white against the black leather sofa.

'Shall we go to bed?' I said.

I could feel him pull away. 'It's no good, I can't do it,' he said.

'I don't mean sex,' I said, 'we could just hold each other.'

'I need another drink,' he said. 'I keep thinking what those women say I did to them, and it's come between me and you.'

'But you didn't rape anyone. You most likely don't even know these women. They've crawled out of nowhere to create some drama for themselves.'

'I'm so confused, Sara, I don't know what's happening to me. But I can't make love to you.'

I didn't know what to say. At last he'd stopped trying to pretend. On one level, I couldn't help feeling devastated at his rejection; on another, I was full of pity for him. Both reactions, though, made me more than ever bitterly angry at his accuser.

'It doesn't matter,' I said. 'It'll pass. Of course you're bound to feel the way you do.'

I said that, but at the same time it didn't help me. I didn't know what to do. The only way I could fight now was to put this horrible thing to one side and concentrate on what was real and good about our relationship. But I couldn't do it alone; Simon had to make an effort too, and I couldn't help asking myself if he could. Was it in him to fight? Did he actually have any inner resources? Did he have anything to fall back on now? He didn't read or take any interest in politics, not even in sport, not in anything at all; he simply sat and drank himself into a stupor watching children's television waiting for me to come home.

And I found myself asking: Who is this person when he's not a full-time TV personality?

Simon stood up. 'I don't know about you,' he said, 'but I could do with another drink.'

'I could do with several,' I said. 'Let's get drunk.'

'Not you, you've got to get to work tomorrow.'

'I'll call in sick. I feel sick. I can't leave you alone now.'

Simon poured more vodka into his glass and swallowed it. Then he poured himself another.

'You mustn't do anything because of me, Sara. You've got to carry on with your life as if this isn't happening.'

I wanted to shout at him, how do I do that?

'Don't worry about me,' I said. 'I'll carry on as usual. It's just today that I want to spend the time with you. We've got to talk. It's important. You're the most important part of my life. You always will be. Nothing's changed for me there.'

If only that were true, but I knew it wasn't. The balance of our relationship was altered for ever. When I'd first met Simon, I'd taken him for a tough working-class northern lad quite different from the boys I'd grown up with in a West County village full of affluent commuters and retired professionals. He'd been the one who could cope when things were tough, who knew what to do. He was never at a loss. He'd had what Frank called 'street-cred in spades', enough for both of us, I'd thought.

But that was all changed now. He couldn't cope. Not any more he couldn't.

At last he said, 'I can't talk about it. Try to understand. If we talk about it, you and me, it'll take over our relationship. I've got Mal to talk to, and the solicitor, thanks to you. I got the solicitor because of you; you told me to and I did.' He was drunk and rambling. He said, 'I can talk to them because it's a professional question, and only about me. Talking between you and me about this nightmare would put it out of control.'

He glanced at me with bleary eyes, then looked away. He went on in a low, disconnected mumble which frightened me. 'If I say anything about it to you,' he said, 'it'll make it real. I don't want this to be part of us. It's nothing to do with us. This is *my* problem. Someone hates me so much they'd make up that horrible thing about me. And then all those people I don't even remember ever meeting have turned against me and said . . .' He stopped. Then he said, 'I can't face it.'

I took his hand. He put down the glass of vodka and pulled me to him. With my head on his shoulder, I said, 'I don't want to make you talk about it. I know you didn't do it, that's all there is to say. But we've got to talk about what we're going to do afterwards. What I want to do is make plans for us, for the future.'

He hugged me tight, so tight I could scarcely breathe. I had to pull away and sit up. I gave him back his glass of vodka.

'First of all,' I said, 'I want to come out of hiding. We love each other. I want us to announce our engagement and set a wedding date for after the trial. I want us to have a baby.'

'What?'

'We'll be normal then, a normal family. I want your baby, Simon.'

I heard him take a deep breath. 'Did you say what I think you did?'

'You know I did.'

I'd expected an extreme reaction, some sort of emotion. I thought maybe he was too drunk to take in what I'd said, but when he spoke he sounded sober, like a man in a business meeting.

'Sara, think what you're saying. How can we bring a child

into all this? It wouldn't be fair to it or you. There's a good chance I'd be in prison for most of its childhood.'

I couldn't accept the idea that he might go to jail. I said, 'Don't you see, it would be something positive we could do? Oh, Simon, I really want us to have a baby.'

'As a token of my innocence?' He laughed to show he was joking.

'I know you're innocent. Soon everyone will. Then we'll be together for the rest of our lives. I don't want to waste any more time.'

He said, and he still sounded like a business man, 'You're not thinking this through, Sara. How could we have a child? Even if I'm not in jail, it's bound to take a while to rebuild my career . . .'

'You're saying being a dad would be bad for your image?'

I could hear how bitter I sounded. I felt bitter. I'd expected him at least to be a bit excited, even – did I dare to hope? – grateful. I wanted to say that being a dad was the best way he could rehabilitate himself with the public. Then I was ashamed that such a thought could even enter my head. An innocent and happy thing like having a baby had nothing to do with sordid exploitation even for Simon's advantage.

I said, and I could hear how brutal I sounded, 'You're inno-cent, but you're not going to be able to carry on where you were when you were so rudely interrupted. You know you're not going to be Mr Clean for a while, for quite a while.'

I saw him wince. I wished I hadn't said it. I hadn't known I even thought it until it came blurting out.

'I don't think you've really thought all this through,' Simon repeated. 'But no, Sara, I appreciate the offer, but at the moment I don't think it's a good idea for either of us. The way things are, the great British public would probably think it was part of a publicity stunt to get me back in their good books.'

Because I hated myself for thinking just that, I lashed out, hissing at him, 'So you're going to let our private lives be dictated by the public and the press and the police and anybody at all except you and me?'

'Sara, think about this . . .'

'I have. To hell with what's happening now, I want us to have a real life together afterwards. I want us to be a normal family.' Then I added, and again I could hear how bitter I sounded, 'But next time I'll run it by the people at the office before I talk to you. Thanks, Simon.'

I burst into tears. But in the back of my mind, even as I was weeping tears of genuine sorrow for myself, for Simon, and the baby we might have had, I asked myself what made me do that?

And I knew the answer was that I could see what was coming and I didn't know how to escape.

I hadn't bargained on any of this, and it wasn't what I wanted to do with my life.

I shoved the thought aside. This wasn't helping anybody. All I'd wanted was to make something happen.

There was silence. Then Simon began to weep.

I didn't know what to do; I was way out of my depth.

'I love you,' I said, again and again. I was scared. I didn't dare touch him. My love was all I had to offer and it wasn't nearly enough.

He was trying to pull himself together. I felt oddly detached, looking at him.

It was seeing the emperor without his clothes. The Simon who had seemed invulnerable, so powerful and sure of himself, was weak and frightened and . . . alien. I didn't know him.

And then he blew his nose, laughed, a little shakily, and kissed my hand.

'I love you, too,' he said. 'Which is why I must regretfully decline your offer.' He wiped a tear from my cheek with his finger. 'Sara, don't you see you can't get involved in all this? This business mustn't ruin you as well as me. I shouldn't even be here. It was insane of me to move in on you like this.'

'But—'

'Sure, announcing our engagement would show the world that one wonderful, attractive, successful woman believes I didn't rape anyone, but don't you see what that would mean to you? That's what you'd *be* afterwards. If I'm found guilty, you'd be branded the woman who stood up for that TV rapist. You'd never live it down. The tabloids are stronger than you are and they'd never let go. I can't let that happen.'

I was silent for a moment.

Then I said, 'Do I take that as a refusal of my proposal, then?'

I smiled, but I was shaken. I couldn't free myself from that earlier image of him, helpless and terrified. It wasn't going to be easy to come to terms with that. I was ashamed that I felt threatened by the scale of his need for me. It was as though the Simon I loved had been broken, maybe beyond repair. I wasn't sure I could cope with being responsible for mending him. Of course I wanted to, but suppose I wasn't strong enough, what would happen to him then?

Even thinking that way made me feel guilty. I loved him. I'd loved him from the moment we met. I'd loved him in spite of the difficulties his lifestyle had caused for both of us. I could laugh off the young girls who mobbed him in the street; the women who offered themselves to him wherever he went; the way he played up to all of it, now flirting, now fleeing. That was Simon. But now all that had gone. People would still stare at him in the street if he went out, but now there'd be nothing but hostility, loud whispers that there was no smoke without fire; that the TV company must've thought he was guilty to sack him, they must know; and why would any woman say he did if he didn't? It took a lot of courage for a woman to come forward. . . . Everyone knew the sort of things that got said, I'd said them myself about other people; but now it was Simon who'd be the object of those whispers, and I knew they'd got it wrong.

It wouldn't only be Simon they'd talk about, either. However much I told him I wanted to defy the lot of them and tell the world about our relationship, I dreaded doing it. I'd be proof of the depths to which he was reduced. They'd laugh at me, say I was the best he could do now, that there'd been a time when Simon West could take his pick of the best-looking women in the world and he was now reduced to me. I'd be the booby prize. And, even worse, Simon might come to agree with them; he wasn't used to bucking public opinion.

I tried to tell myself it wouldn't happen, and if it did, I'd take it, but would I? I didn't think I could. That kind of thing could destroy every scrap of confidence I'd got.

You needed to be confident in yourself when someone really needed you. I was all Simon had to defend himself against unfamiliar empty hours and the sudden isolation of disgrace. I'd be all right as long as I was angry at the unfairness of it all, but that took the sort of self-belief that I could easily lose.

I started then to think about the woman who'd done this to Simon. And to me, too; she'd done it to me as well. I thought about her all the time. I was angry that this sad bitch was dictating to us, Simon and me. And nothing could touch her. I didn't even like to ask him what he knew about her because she'd got legal anonymity; he'd know I'd been abusing my job to find out that her name was Midgley. She was someone I'd never heard of, but she had brought our lives crashing down in ruins. Why? Did she know what she'd done? Was she enjoying it, the sense of power? If she was some sort of sicko who thought she was in love with Simon, she'd only made him hate her. He must hate her. What was she getting out of it, for God's sake?

I was scared how passionately angry I felt against this woman. All my fears for Simon, for myself, and our future together, hardened my hatred for the shadowy Ms Midgley. I wished her all kinds of suffering as punishment. She had to be made to suffer for what she'd done.

The woman became an actual presence in my life. It got so I couldn't do anything without the thought of the accuser being there with me, demanding my attention, taunting me.

I was losing control. There were complaints about my work at the office. Frank gave me an official warning.

'What's got into you?' he said. 'A monkey would do a better job of subbing this stuff than you have. In fact, every single monkey I've got on the staff is doing a better job than you these days.'

There was nothing I could say.

'I'm sorry, Frank,' I muttered.

I was afraid I was going to burst into tears, which he would never forgive.

'Are you sick?' he asked. 'If it's some sort of female problem, take time off. But for Christ's sake, sort it.'

I could think of nothing worse than taking time off now. There'd be just Simon and me, nothing I could hide behind to give myself a break. I felt guilty about it, but I needed work as a way of convincing myself I still had an independent existence outside Simon's suffering and my hatred for his persecutor.

Worse still, because Frank was trying to be kind, I had to fight off an almost overwhelming urge to tell him everything.

I managed to shake my head. 'No, I don't need time off. I'm sorry.'

'You've not got yourself pregnant, or something stupid like

that, have you?' Frank sounded grumpy because he was embarrassed.

'Me? Pregnant?' I said. 'Not on your life.'

'Well, do what you have to,' he said, 'but this can't go on. Now get out of here and let the rest of us get on with bringing out the bloody paper.'

On my way home I parked the car and sat for some time staring at the streetlamps reflected in the river. I opened the car window and felt the cold breeze off the water against my face. There was a faint smell of tar and mud. The tide was coming in and I could hear the murmur of the river lapping against the shore.

'You bitch,' I said aloud to the woman called Midgley, 'I'm not going to let you get away with what you're doing to me and Simon, whoever the hell you are.'

It was a declaration of war.

'I'm going to find out who you are, Ms Midgley, I'm going to hunt you down and then I'm going to make you pay,' I said, and the sudden din of a crowd of seagulls affirmed that vow.

6

Out of my Depth

At last I asked Simon, 'Do you know someone called Midgley?'

I'd given myself so many plausible reasons for not confronting this question that when I did come out with it, I expected some sort of dramatic response from Simon. But he looked puzzled, not surprised.

'Midgley? You mean Karen?'

'I don't know who I mean, do I?'

I wanted to shout at him: I'm talking about the woman who's falsely accusing you of raping her, the anonymous bloody cow who's out to get you, who's ruined your career, who's come between you and me. . . . No, I told myself, don't. Don't go there.

I tried to sound casual, asking, 'So who's Karen Midgley?'

Simon frowned. He wasn't too drunk, but he was drunk enough to be defensive. 'She wasn't a girlfriend, if that's what you're thinking. She was my friend.' His eyes filled and his voice thickened.

Did his emotion mean he knew his 'friend' had betrayed him? Or were his tears pure nostalgia for an innocent affection?

I said nothing and waited for him to go on.

'Karen helped me out once, and I helped her when she was in trouble. It was all a long time ago.' He seemed to be smiling through his tears at the memory of his friend Karen. 'She was a special person,' he said.

'Does she live here? In Castleborough?'

'No. No, she came from some place way out in the country.'

'So where did you meet?'

His memories were obviously causing him no particular pain, or he'd surely have wondered why I kept asking questions.

'I was hosting a TV quiz series in Leeds,' he said. 'She was working at the studio as a researcher on the programme. We used to talk.'

He seemed suddenly to notice that my question wasn't altogether casual. 'What is this, anyway?' he said. 'Why are you asking about Karen?'

I couldn't tell anything from his tone. I forced myself to sound uninterested.

'Oh, her name came up. Someone in the office mentioned her.'

I looked at him, trying to read his face. Did he know what she'd done? He must know it was her.

But his expression was blank, although his hand shook as he lit a cigarette. 'But why did you connect her with me?' he asked.

'Your name came up too.'

'So you gossip about me with those yobs you work with? That's nice. I think I liked it better when I was a household name, you get talked about by a better class of moron.'

I lost my temper then. I shouted at him, 'I liked it better then, too. Then all they talked about was the dirty little tarts you were screwing. Now it's nothing but who's the latest bitch who says you raped her.'

Simon went white. He jumped up and came to me, putting his arms around me.

'Sara, don't,' he said. 'Stop it, please. I'm so sorry. I never thought. I didn't realize. Please, we mustn't quarrel. I can't bear it if we quarrel.'

I couldn't help thinking, *you* can't bear it? *You!* It's all about you, isn't it? What about me? Haven't you any idea what this is like for me?

I knew I was being unfair but I couldn't stop myself, although of course it *was* all about him. But I was paying a price for loving him, too, except he didn't seem to realize.

A voice in my head said, you didn't have to fall in love with him, did you?

As if I'd had any choice. It had happened, love at first sight. But this nightmare wasn't his fault. I told myself he didn't ask women to throw themselves at him. But in a way he did, didn't he? He liked being a sex symbol.

The sight of him standing there with his hands held out to me, his eyes full of need for me, filled me again with that hateful fear that he was a stranger now. I was afraid, too, that on my own I couldn't give him what he needed. I wouldn't get any help from him. He was past being able to help me.

I took a deep breath and did my best to smile. 'Forget it,' I told him, 'we mustn't fight. I didn't mean it. It's just some-times . . .'

'I know,' he said. He turned away to refill his glass and went to stare out of the window. He didn't look at me as he said, 'I talked to Mal again this morning.'

'And?'

'One advertising campaign and a charity gala bite the dust.'

'Bastards,' I snarled. Anger seemed the only way to mask my fear for him. I shouted, 'Whatever happened to innocent until proven guilty? When this is over you may be able to sue them for breach of contract.'

'That's what Mal said. But you can't blame them. They can't afford to offend the paying public, can they?'

His voice sounded carefully reasonable, but all the life had died out of it.

I began to rage at those faceless, nameless executives who held our future in their manicured hands. 'It's not fair. No one even knows who this woman is accusing you, and yet the papers have made you into a public enemy. What's she getting out of it?'

I stopped myself from using Karen Midgley's name. I didn't want to upset Simon again. He was obviously in denial, refusing to face what someone he'd trusted as an old friend was doing to him.

'It's a bandwagon,' he said, and he sounded sad, not bitter. 'They're attention-seeking, I suppose. Or does it give them a sense of power, do you think? Simply being able to do it. What the hell! Mal didn't sound as though he fancies his chances of being paid this month – or this year, come to that. I've nothing coming in.'

'I'd like to kill her,' I said.

'Don't let anyone hear you say that,' Simon said, 'the cops will charge you with conspiracy to murder or something. It won't help anything if we're both in jail.'

It was a brief flash of the old Simon. I forced myself to laugh. 'I'll get us something to eat,' I said. 'Then I'll have to go to work. One of us had better earn something.'

I'd meant it to be lighthearted, sort of us against the

world, and it slipped out before I'd thought how it sounded. I saw him flinch. Idiot, I told myself, then, not knowing what to say or do to take it back, I went into the kitchen to prepare one of his favourites, spaghetti with basil and tomato sauce. At least, I hoped he'd feel better once he'd got some good hot food inside him. I sounded so like my mother to myself, I had to smile in spite of everything.

'It's too much,' Simon said when I brought him the food on a tray. 'I can't face a pile of food like that.'

I nearly threw the spaghetti in his drunken face. I don't know why I felt so hurt. It's not as if I'd any illusions about my cooking skills; it wouldn't be the first time Simon had been rude about my culinary offerings. But it seemed to me at that moment that food was all the comfort I could offer Simon, and he rejected it with contempt.

I sat down and started to eat my own meal rather than burst into tears.

'You eat too much,' Simon said, 'it's bad for you.'

Frank's voice echoed in my head, asking me in that embarrassed way if I was pregnant. It was true I was putting on weight. Perhaps anyone else going through what was happening to Simon would worry themselves thin, but I was the opposite, I ate myself silly because I didn't know what else to do. I suppose it was a stupid form of escapism, but however much I told myself I'd cut back, when it came down to it I never thought what I was doing till I'd scoffed the lot.

And then a chilling thought struck me. Could Simon think I was doing it to make myself as unattractive as possible because subconsciously I wanted to drive him away so I could get out of this situation without feeling guilty? He couldn't think that. Could I have thought it if there weren't a grain of truth in it? No, how could I even think such a thing? It *wasn't* that.

I was out of my depth. I couldn't cope.

7

The Graduate Course in Rape

At work, Frank gave me a story about Simon to edit for the front page of the first edition. There was no way out, short of fainting away. It wasn't as if I hadn't been warned about my work; if I refused, he'd fire me.

'Here's the headline,' he said, 'cut it to fit. Along the lines of *"Shamed Star out in the Cold"*. The story's about the latest gurgle as his career goes down the pan.'

'Don't you think we should be a bit careful here?' I said. 'I mean, he may not be found guilty. He might have a case for damages if we make things worse for him.'

Frank hooted with laughter. 'What's got into you, woman?' he demanded. 'Whoever got anywhere in newspapers by letting the lack of a guilty verdict stand in the way of a good story? You know the score, get on with it.'

'You needn't sound so pleased about it,' I said.

The girl sitting at the computer screen next to mine laughed. 'It couldn't have happened to a nastier little shit, though, could it?' she said.

'Oh, you know him well, do you?' I asked with heavy sarcasm.

This girl's name was Fortuny, and I'd always disliked her for that. Surely anyone worth their salt with a name like that would pretend they were really called Helen or Susan or something equally unpretentious? But it wasn't only her stupid name I objected to about Fortuny: I disliked the virtuous and self-satisfied statement of her cosmetic-free pale skin, her wispy hair, her colourless eyes magnified behind wire-rimmed spectacles, and the long denim skirts she always wore with flimsy flowing tops and flat moccasins. There was something long-suffering and victimized about her that struck me as positively aggressive. And I also resented it that I was apparently the only person in the world who didn't see the girl as some kind of sweet-natured saint. Even Frank did.

Then this vision of virtue smiled the smile of one who knew better. She said, 'My sister queued all night in the rain to see him last year and when he turned up he didn't even give autographs. Who does he think he is, I'd like to know?'

'If your sister looks anything like you, I'm surprised he didn't turn and run,' I muttered, but under my breath.

I worked for a while in silence. Then I asked, 'Do you think he did it?'

'Of course he did it,' Fortuny said. 'Arrogant brute, thinks he's only got to click his fingers and women will do anything he wants. Well, he's got another think coming now.'

'Suppose he didn't?'

'Do it? He must've done it. You've only got to look at him to know the sort of man he is. Have you ever looked at his eyes? Anyone who looked at his eyes could tell he was a rapist. Anyway, why would any woman say he had if he hadn't? Surely you don't think his poor victim would lie?'

I had to laugh at that. 'It wouldn't be the first time,' I said.

Fortuny began to get angry. 'What kind of woman are you? Calling her a liar? Next thing you'll be saying *he's* the victim. Why are you defending someone like him? Whose side are you on, anyway?'

'What about the side of truth? Or even facts?' I said, and I resented being made to sound pompous.

Fortuny stared at me in disbelief.

So I changed the subject. 'What've you got?' I asked. 'Anything good?'

Fortuny pulled a face. 'What about *"Has-been Visits Old Haunts"*,' she said.

'What's that about?'

'Marta Blane's paying a visit to her old school pals in our great city.'

I pretended ignorance. 'Who or what is Marta Blane?'

'Oh, you must know who she is. She went to America and was a singer and a movie actress there for a while. But before that she wanted to marry Simon West. He took out an injunction to stop her going anywhere near him. We wouldn't be interested in her now if he wasn't in the news. She says she's bringing the new love of her life, who's a bit-part actor called Boris something or other, home to meet the family, but I bet you anything she's here because Hollywood is as unwelcoming now as Simon West was in the old days. And it would be a good story to find out what Marta thinks of what's happening to her great love now. She must've noticed signs of him being a pervert. There'd have been little things she'd remember which she'd know now were the signs of a rapist. Things he said or did in bed which would've revealed the truth to someone in the know.'

'Someone in the know? Is that part of the graduate course in rape?' I said. 'Can you tell by the look in the eyes and the way they stand or walk? Anyway, wouldn't it be *sub judice*? Prejudicing a fair trial and all that? Where's she staying?'

'Where d'you think – The Grand. The family home's a little too humble now for our Marta, in decline or not. She's got to keep up appearances, make it look like she's still doing well. I think it'd be worth having someone hang around to see if she tries to see Simon. I think I'll suggest it to Frank.'

'You know, you're right,' I said. 'I tell you what, I'm off soon. I'm having a drink with someone in The Grand tonight. I'll keep my eyes peeled and give you a ring if anything happens. You could do the story for the second edition.'

Fortuny looked suspicious. 'What's in it for you?'

'Not a thing. Just doing a favour for a fellow female.'

I could see she suspected my motives. It had never occurred to me before that Fortuny didn't like me any more than I liked her, but a sub-editor's only chance of a byline was when a story broke late at night and the sub put it together for the last edition. Someone as ambitious as Fortuny would give a lot for a byline.

'It's my idea,' she said, 'so I get the byline, right?'

'It's all yours,' I said. Let her hope, but I'd no intention of getting anything for the paper from Marta Blane.

Fortuny was a bitch and I didn't like the way she was trying to trash Marta Blane. Marta might not be a big star, but she'd gone on to Hollywood and she'd made a few films with big name actors in them; she was light years ahead of Fortuny anyway.

Light years ahead of me, too.

8

Confronting Ghosts and Demons

The Grand Hotel had seen better days, but it was still imposing in its provincial respectability. It was so old-fashioned that women were supposed to be accompanied in the public rooms. I got some hard looks from the reception desk when I sat down in the lobby to wait for Marta Blane, but security apparently decided I looked too scruffy to be a prostitute and let me be.

I found it odd contriving a meeting with Marta Blane, a stranger I knew too well because of her fling with Simon. In the early days of our relationship, mine and Simon's, Marta had loomed large for me. I'd listened to two or three of her albums and seen her films and I'd read all the cuttings about her romance with Simon in the newspaper library. There were a lot of those, because Marta's pursuit of Simon had been a big local story which made the nationals. There'd been photographs as well, lots of photographs of the two of them, first of their fairy-tale show-business romance, then, later, of love gone sour.

So I knew Marta Blane the moment I saw her come into

the lobby. She was preoccupied as she crossed the marble foyer, searching in her handbag for something. For a moment, I was disappointed. I'd wanted to feel proud that Simon loved me, not her. Now she didn't look so marvellous, or so much more beautiful than me. She was dark and certainly glamorous, but at first sight she seemed to me quite ordinary.

And then I couldn't understand how I could have been so mistaken. As she approached the reception desk, it was as though a light was switched on inside her. She was suddenly radiant. Marta Blane was glorious: her hair gleamed, her skin glowed; she walked, I thought, like some queen, Cleopatra perhaps, or Nefertiti, striding through the desert.

I was suddenly embarrassed that I could have compared myself with her, aware of my dirty hair and baggy clothes. But this was not why I hesitated to approach her. I held back because Marta Blane was alone. I'd expected an entourage of minders and publicity people. I knew how to deal with them. And on top of that, Marta was obviously off-duty, an ordinary person wearing jeans and a sweater just like me, and I was suddenly aware that I was intruding on a real person.

She went across to the lifts. She was reading a note she'd been handed at reception.

I couldn't give up now. I'd nothing to lose.

I marched straight up to her.

'My name's Sara Soames,' I said. 'You don't know me, but please can I speak to you for a moment?'

Marta Blane stared at me, curious rather than hostile.

'It's about Simon West,' I said.

The famous trademark blue eyes met mine.

'You'd better come up to the suite with me,' she said. Her voice sounded like music. 'Boris is jet-lagged. He's gone to bed. We can talk in the sitting-room.'

She sounded non-committal, but not unfriendly.

We took the lift to the penthouse suite in silence.

I followed Marta into a room full of over-stuffed pastel armchairs and pleated oyster silk lampshades. Before I'd even closed the door, she'd kicked off her shoes and poured herself a drink from the mini bar. I noticed that the dark red varnish on her toenails was chipped.

'Whisky?' she asked, holding up a bottle of malt. 'It's that or champagne.'

'Whisky's fine. Thanks.'

Marta sat cross-legged on the floor. I perched on the slippery edge of one of the chairs.

She fixed me with the blue stare. 'So what's this about? Where is Simon?'

'You know what's happened?'

Marta nodded. 'I've read the papers.'

I swallowed my drink in one gulp and took a deep breath.

'I'm his girlfriend,' I said.

She didn't react.

'Funny,' I said, 'you're the first person I've ever said that to. We've been together for eighteen months. We kept it a secret, and now he won't let me come out and stand up for him. He needs help, though. Of course, what this woman and the others are saying isn't true. But before he's even been found guilty, he's lost his job and there's no money and no work, and the police haven't even decided yet to go ahead with a trial . . .'

Marta put up her hand to stop the torrent of words.

'OK, I know all that,' she said. 'But what do you think I can do to help? I haven't even seen him for years.'

'Do you know Karen Midgley?'

'Karen?' Marta looked startled, then she began to laugh. 'What's Karen got to do with it?'

61

'Who is she? Do you know about her?'

'OK, you wouldn't be here if you didn't know about Simon and me. But you won't know that Simon used Karen to get rid of me. I was besotted with him, you know, and I made a fool of myself. It's hard to believe that now. I look back at myself then and try to imagine why I was so obsessed by him. He was incredibly vain and so up his own backside, I can see now he didn't really exist as a real person. I suppose you'd say I would say that *now*.'

She was still the bitter woman scorned, I told myself. But I recognized some truth in what she said, on a superficial, naive level anyway, and I smiled at her to go on. Simon was vain, as vain as any girl, but I saw it as funny, an amusing foible of the love object.

What I wanted to know was more about Karen Midgley.

'And what happened then?' I asked.

'Simon tried to choke me off. OK, he and I lived together for a while, about three months. Then he threw me out. It was never serious for him, but it was for me. I wanted to marry him. It's funny to think of now, but I've never wanted anything in the world more than I wanted to marry him.'

Marta hesitated, the deep-blue eyes looking into the distance. Then she laughed. It seemed to me that Marta Blane was no longer emotionally connected to the woman she'd been then, it was as if she were describing a character she'd once played in a movie, and that a humble low-budget production.

She went on, 'Actually, I suppose I stalked him. I've had a bit of the same thing myself since, and I know now how he must've felt. You get terrified. It's no different for men, he must've felt like that too. In the end he told me that he and Karen were an item. I didn't want to believe it. He made me go round to their place and meet her. OK, she was living there. I checked that out. They didn't seem like lovers to me, but she was pregnant, so I couldn't doubt it.'

Marta's big blue eyes took on a misty look as she remembered. 'She wasn't his type at all,' she said, 'a real country bumpkin, practically straw in her hair. I don't think she even knew he was famous.'

But I'd heard only that one word. *Pregnant*. Karen Midgley had been pregnant.

My head swam. If I hadn't been sitting down, I'd have fallen.

I saw the funny look Marta Blane gave me, and made an effort to pull myself together.

'Do you know what she's doing now?' I asked. 'Or where she lives? Anything?'

Marta looked puzzled. She said, 'Look, I don't know you, or what you're after. Why are you asking about Karen?'

Before I could say anything, the beautiful eyes opened wide. She looked startled.

'My God,' she said, 'you think Karen's the rape victim – alleged rape victim? You think she's the one making these charges against him, don't you?'

I didn't answer.

Marta's eyes narrowed. 'I wonder . . . are you sure?' She shrugged. 'OK, for what it's worth I did check her out, but it's some time ago now. She came from somewhere in the sticks near a village towards the Scottish border. Brockley, or Brockdale, a name starting with Brock, anyway. Brockbeck, that was it. She may still be there. Those places are like closed communities, everyone related to everyone else. Karen was a bit simple, you know, kind of fey. Not a bit like the other television people Simon was involved with. As I said, I couldn't see what she and Simon could have in common. She was a good-looking girl, but not all that good-looking.'

Marta looked at me and I knew that she was finding me also not all that good-looking, in fact not good-looking at all.

I flushed.

'I thought she might be able to help, that's all,' I said. 'Thanks for talking to me.'

'No problem,' Marta said. 'Is that it?'

'Yes, that's it.'

'I thought you might want to know that I don't think Simon could rape anyone.'

I could see that Marta was curious about me. The famous blue eyes met mine. It felt like staring into searchlights on a stage.

'No,' I said. 'I know he didn't do it. I don't need you to tell me that. Why should I?'

'Oh,' Marta said, 'for when the doubts creep in at three o'clock in the morning.'

'No,' I said, 'I don't have doubts. Not at any hour.'

I walked down the stairs rather than take the lift. I wanted a moment to myself to take in what Marta Blane had told me. But I'd need more time to consider what she'd said, and if it changed anything.

I couldn't think clearly about this at home, any more than at work. I needed neutral territory, and the hotel bar provided that. I decided to have a quiet drink before going home.

I saw Simon at once as I walked into the cocktail bar. Actually, my first thought was that the blond hunk about to sit down at a corner table with a flashy little fellow in a rather beautiful pin-stripe suit looked a lot like Simon. Then I saw the blond hunk was Simon, having an earnest conversation with his odd little sidekick.

Three middle-aged women having coffee and liqueurs at the next table got up to go as the two men sat down.

'I don't know about you two,' one of the women said to

her friends in a loud voice, 'but I don't feel safe in a place that's willing to serve a man like that.'

She could've been Fortuny's mother, I thought, she'd got that same belligerent put-upon girliness.

Another, a well-groomed woman showing signs of being due another Botox treatment, gathered her belongings to go.

'I don't know what the world's coming to,' she said, 'you don't expect to meet perverts in a hotel like this, not at these prices.'

I wanted to rush over and slap their stupid, self-satisfied faces. Instead, I walked slowly across the blood-coloured carpet to meet them as they moved away from Simon and his friend.

'Oh, good,' I said to them, 'you're going. I'm glad to see this hotel hasn't totally abandoned its old standards. At least they're still throwing out the old tarts who come in off the street to pick up businessmen.'

I smiled as the women began to bluster. 'The night's still young, you might still find the odd blind drunk down at the station if you hurry,' I added in a kindly voice.

Simon's flashy friend was staring at this little spectacle. Simon had turned his back on us.

I moved towards him, slightly apologetic for making a scene in such a place, but also glad that I'd been able to defend him so publicly.

He blanked me. He gave no sign of recognizing me at all. His friend, flustered, leaned across the low, glass-topped table with a flash of diamond ring and expensive watch as he said to Simon, 'Who were those women? At least the fierce young fat one obviously doesn't believe what she reads in the newspapers. Do you want to go somewhere else?'

'God knows who they were,' Simon said. 'But let's get out of here.'

He got up and ignored me while he waited for the little man in the pin-stripe suit, then they both walked together out of the bar. The little man gave me an embarrassed smile as he went, obviously worried about what the fierce young fat one might do next.

9

Clutching at Straws

Believe it or not, neither Simon nor I mentioned what had happened in the hotel. I went home and waited for him to come back and have it out. I expected him to apologize. At least I thought, he should explain why he'd blanked me. I knew he'd say he didn't want to acknowledge me where a reporter could be lurking; it had been for my own good. That wouldn't have been a good enough excuse, but it would've been better than the nothing I got. But when he came home and carried on as though nothing had happened, I started to be afraid of the inevitable emotional scene if I forced him to talk about it. So I let it drift. I didn't want to provoke him.

Thinking about it, though, I decided he must have thought I'd followed him to the hotel, spying on him. Did he think I didn't trust him after all we'd been through? Actually, what I really thought was, didn't he trust me after all I'd done for him, but I couldn't admit that even to myself. I was humiliated enough by what had happened in that bloody hotel and then I was angry that in spite of everything he obviously understood me so little.

Why did I let him treat me like that? I wouldn't have taken it from anyone else. But then I wasn't scared of losing anyone else. I couldn't help loving Simon whatever he did. It might have been pathetic, but I couldn't see any point in my life without him. I knew I should have confronted him, but I didn't want to explain how I'd gone to see Marta Blane, and why. I tried to put the incident behind me and concentrate on other things. Or rather, on one other thing: Karen Midgley.

Meeting Marta Blane had turned my curiosity about Karen Midgley into something like an obsession. There were so many unanswered questions, and no one to ask for answers. Except Simon, of course, but for the time being I couldn't see a way of bringing up the subject. Most likely he'd simply refuse to talk about it, or even fly off the handle. Increasingly, there seemed to be nothing I could ask him that he was prepared to talk about. I tried to avoid bringing up anything that might tip him into one of his moods, but I couldn't get away from worrying that even when we'd been really close in the past, Simon had never told me about the child he'd had with Karen Midgley. But I was afraid to force the issue – any issue.

For a start, I didn't have to be a mind reader to know I wasn't going to get anywhere talking to him about something important unless he was sober, and these days, he was scarcely ever sober.

I told myself he needed the drink to get through the awful waiting, that it would be different when there was something definite, but that was just an excuse.

I was actually a little afraid of him the way he was. His hopelessness was frightening; it was so unlike him. He was angry at the people he knew because they couldn't stop what was happening to him, and at the same time he was consumed with hatred for everyone he didn't know because they were enjoying the spectacle of his destruction. I couldn't help him. My efforts at being supportive or positive irritated him. And, of course, his constant drinking made him more unreasonable than ever.

So my growing obsession with Karen Midgley was a defence mechanism. Finding out about Simon's alleged victim was a way to take some form of positive action. It was part of fighting back against Simon's passiveness. That drove me mad. I understood his drinking and his self-pity, but sometimes I longed to shout at him to fight back, *do* something, get out and look for any kind of work instead of giving up because one door had been slammed in his face.

But realistically I knew there wasn't anything he could do, and in my heart I knew it wouldn't help if he did, no one wanted him now. Being turned down would simply increase his sense of rejection. He was lost, waiting to be told what to do. And what could I tell him? I didn't know. Nothing I said was any use.

I'd say, 'You should get out of the house, at least you could keep in touch with your friends.'

'Friends? What friends? They were friends with the celebrity Simon West. What would we have to say to each other now he's dead and buried?'

'There's going to be life after the trial,' I said. I wanted to slap him. I was late for work, and he was already well on the way to getting drunk again, but I was frightened to seem impatient to get away.

So the barrier between us kept growing. We neither of us had anyone else to turn to, and, aware of that, I suppose each tried not to distress the other. He shut me out. I put off telling him that I'd seen Marta; I didn't mention Karen Midgley's name; I shied away from questions about pregnancy, any pregnancy. I felt a kind of noose tightening around everything I said to him. There seemed to be more and more subjects I couldn't bring up in conversation with him. We were left with nothing to say to each other.

In my head I said things to Simon I couldn't say to his face. 'You can't let things go on like this', I told him. 'What kind of person are you?' I tried to answer the question for him, but I'd nothing to say. He wasn't a person at all, he'd been a celebrity and at that moment he didn't really exist. There was no one there to get through to. That was something else I didn't want to think about.

Sometimes I looked into the blank, bleary eyes, which had once been so thrillingly clear blue, searching for the man I loved. Occasionally, too, I fancied I caught a glimpse of him behind the blank screen, my Simon desperate, begging for help.

Even at such moments, though, I had the terrifying feeling that it was only the image of the man I loved in pain, because that was what he was, an image.

I loved him, that hadn't changed, and it wouldn't. It was only that I'd never had to ask myself before exactly who it was I loved, and why I loved him. I knew I wasn't being fair. After all, how would anyone else behave if someone falsely accused them of rape? They'd be the same as Simon. Still, it wasn't any good, when I tried to reach out to him – he wasn't there.

Simon seemed to be struggling just as much to hold on to the me of our love before he'd been arrested. He didn't tell me what was happening. When he was given a date for the trial, I found out about it at work. It was the front page lead throughout the early editions, until a crowded holiday jet crash-landed at Castleborough Airport. I kept silent, waiting for Simon to feel he could tell me himself, but he didn't.

It got harder than ever to get close to him. We talked about the weather, about Castleborough United's chances of winning the Football League, or the doings of Castleborough's politicians, anything at all that skirted round the subject that actually occupied us both. I was even careful not to touch him now. It was painfully obvious he didn't want me near him. It was as though when I went close to him his first reaction was to avoid contact. I told myself that what had happened had made him wary of all women, so even with me there was a split second before his brain registered that I wasn't an enemy. But I couldn't quite overcome how that not quite hidden recoil of his hurt me.

Rather than talk to me, he was spending hours on the telephone to his agent, Mal. I could tell from the one-sided conversations I overheard that Mal was trying to get him off the phone.

Then Mal rang me at work.

'There's nothing I can do,' he said. 'Can you get him to take that in? I've done all I can. I've got to earn a living. He's always on the phone. Paying clients can't get through to me.'

There was nothing I could say.

Except blame Karen. I'd begun to think of Karen by her first name, as though I actually knew her.

Everything came down to Karen. Everything was her fault. Night after night, I lay awake planning revenge on her. I plotted ways to hurt her. The fantasizing helped me not to think of what lay ahead for Simon. And for me.

Sometimes it was as though he thought he might be guilty. As the one person whose belief in his innocence was absolute, I became suspect. His trust in me was corroded as his confidence melted away.

And it was Karen's fault.

A week before the trial, I couldn't bear it any longer. I had to *do* something. Simon had moved back to his apartment, now discreetly for sale. I hadn't seen him for days. On the phone, I'd offered to go over; I'd asked him to my place, but he always put me off. 'I'm not very good company at the moment,' he said. 'I don't want you to have to see me this way.' And when I said I didn't mind, he simply told me, 'I'd rather be alone.'

But he rang me all the time. It was embarrassing. I deliberately left my mobile at home because he rang constantly when I was supposed to be working. I told him not to. Frank was making barbed comments about putting me on half pay because I only worked part-time.

'Don't call me at work,' I begged Simon, 'I could lose my job. They don't like us to have personal calls.'

'But I need to talk to you,' he said. 'You're the only person I can talk to.'

If only. . . . But he didn't talk, he babbled like Lear's Fool.

'It's not just your calls,' I told him, 'it's the way they make me feel afterwards. I can't concentrate on what I'm doing.'

'I'm sorry,' he said, sounding stricken, 'I don't want to be a burden.'

So I left the mobile at home. I got the switchboard to say I was out to anyone who phoned me at the office. I spent the time instead thinking of Simon waiting alone. I felt horribly guilty. So then I'd ring him.

Every night when I got home, my phone would be ringing. If I ignored it, it would ring again and again through the night. Sometimes, when he called and I was in bed, I'd doze off in the long silences between his attempts to speak to me. I'd wake up with a start not sure if he'd said anything I should answer. My efforts to keep up bright, meaningless, chatter had died away from lack of response.

It couldn't go on like this. I had to take some sort of action to break the tension. I didn't have to be at home for him to talk to me on the mobile. I wouldn't abandon him, I'd still be there for him, but he wouldn't know where I was.

Frank was only too glad to let me take a few days off.

'About time too,' he muttered. 'Sort it out, woman, whatever it is. Otherwise you're not going to have a job to come back to. Get a grip or go, OK?'

10

Getting to Know the Enemy

I drove out of Castleborough in the early morning, well before the weekday traffic began to build up. Mist still hung above the river and the rising sun caught the top windows of the high-rise flats on the north side of the city so they flared like lighted matches. It was beautiful and I felt tears in my eyes because it was the first time in ages I'd been able to see that things still could be beautiful.

A few heavy lorries trundled down the High Street, taking a short cut through the city centre on their way north before the commuter traffic built up. A corporation refuse cart kerb-crawled in the main shopping area, a team of cheery men wearing enormous gloves sang along to a ballad about late-night love from the radio in the cab of the vehicle. It struck me as an outlandish song in the early morning. Suddenly, absurdly, I felt homesick for the city I was leaving.

And, I admit, for the cheerful, everyday normality I thought I'd lost.

I almost turned back then. But at that instant, a milkman stepped out behind his van without looking and I had to stamp on the brakes and swerve to avoid him. The moment had passed. I drove on, more slowly.

The shops and offices gave way to tree-lined pavement, then the clipped privet hedges of the Victorian and Edwardian villas of the city's original suburbs. After that, I knew I'd be entering unknown territory.

I reckoned that Brockbeck was about ninety miles north-west of Castleborough. In travelling from Castleborough to Brockbeck, I reckoned I'd move out of the world of towns and supermarkets and regular bus routes I was familiar with, into quite another where I'd be in alien country. On the map the Brockbeck area didn't look like the pastoral leafy land-scape I'd known as a child in the West Country; it seemed to be a vast open moorland with few roads, fewer villages, and no towns at all worthy of the name, a place where the tide of human progress had met its match.

If I understood why I was doing this at all, I was hoping everything might fall into place in my mind. But I didn't understand. Simply I had to see Karen Midgley. I wanted to see what sort of woman she was, that was all. It seemed important to know what Karen looked like, who she knew, how she spent her time. I didn't know why it seemed to matter so much. I suppose I had an idea that I'd play detective and expose her lies.

At least I thought if I knew about her I might understand why she'd done what she did.

Most important of all, I wanted to know about the child, Simon's child. I told myself it wasn't the most important thing, but it was really. I had to know why she was doing what she'd done to Simon, her child's father. Once I knew that, perhaps I could do something about it. I wasn't a total idiot, I knew there must have been something between them if she could hate him enough to want to destroy everything for him after all this time, and my life too? Did she know I existed? Perhaps Simon had secretly kept in touch with her because of the kid and told her about me. She could be acting now out of jealousy because of me. But it didn't make any difference to me now if she was more of a victim than a villain, nothing could change the way I hated her for what she'd done.

It had all seemed so simple when I set out. Sensible, even. I'd thought I was doing the sensible thing.

The countryside grew bleaker, and the few frowning grey stone villages seemed more hostile. The landscape intimidated me. It didn't seem to me that the natives were likely to be friendly. I began to doubt my own sanity in coming. What had possessed me? Why was I here? If I found Karen, I couldn't simply approach her. That could be called interfering with a witness, and, if she complained, the police would think I was acting for Simon. They'd make it seem like an admission of his guilt. I couldn't risk that.

But that wasn't why I wanted to see her. I didn't want to talk to her, even. What I wanted was to find a focus for the way I hated her. I couldn't go on hating a shadow. I *needed* to know who my enemy was.

Also – and I couldn't admit the truth even to myself – I wanted to work out a way to make Karen Midgley suffer as Simon and I were now suffering.

But suddenly all this seemed ridiculous. I was wasting my time. I'd almost persuaded myself to turn round and go home when I saw the signpost to Brockbeck. I'd come so far now I might as well drive into the village, just to see where Karen came from. Then I'd go away. I wouldn't try to find her.

Brockbeck itself seemed to scowl at me for coming at all. The gaunt grey village had a grocery shop and post office, and a stern granite Methodist chapel frowning at a rather shamefaced pub, The Black Bull.

I was hungry after my drive. I'd go into the shop to get something to eat. Then I'd go back to Castleborough.

But it was easier to park outside the pub, and I liked the idea of making a small gesture of support for the drinking hole against that disapproving, puritanical church and its stony-faced parish. A quick snack in The Black Bull then, and I'd be on my way.

Inside the pub, the bar was like a factory canteen. The landlord was leaning on the counter talking to two old men who were his only customers. They fell silent as I walked in. The way they stared at me, not exactly hostile but without friendliness, I felt like a traveller from another world, which I suppose I was.

I sat alone by an unlit fire eating a sandwich of shavings of hard cheese between slices of processed bread, and felt them watching me. No one had said a word since I came in.

I finished the sandwich and took the plate back to the bar. The old men stepped back as though I might be infectious. I offered them a drink. They said nothing, but the landlord drew them pints of beer. These they drank, their bleary eyes fixed on me above the rims of the glasses.

'You visiting?' the landlord asked me at last. I found it hard to understand his lilting accent.

'I'm looking for someone who used to work with a friend of mine,' I said.

'Who's that, then?' one old man asked.

'Karen Midgley,' I said.

'Oh, Karen,' said the landlord.

'Do you know her?'

'Wouldn't say that,' said one old man.

'Not *know*,' said the other, 'no, not know her.'

'Not like you'd know her ma,' said the first.

The second laughed, a sound like dry leaves in a gale. They were teasing the stranger.

'Her ma's late today,' the landlord said. 'Usually here by now.'

'She'll be here soon,' the first old man said. 'She'll tell you where Karen's at.'

I hadn't reckoned on this. I knew I should leave at once, but I was afraid that might make them suspicious.

Anyway, it was too late.

'Here's Jean now,' the landlord said, pouring whisky into a glass. 'First one's on the house,' he said.

Jean Midgley, Karen's mother, was an unexpected sight in this stern, grey place. She was already drunk. She lurched across the room on perilously high heels. An inch or so of pale-grey roots made her frizz of virulent bleached yellow hair look like a lop-sided halo. A cartoon mouth in bright scarlet lipstick did not quite follow the outline of her own lips, so when she spoke the sound seemed to come from somewhere else, like a ventriloquist's dummy.

The two old men helped her to climb on to a stool between them at the bar. She drained the whisky and pushed the empty glass forward for the landlord to refill it.

I was startled. I hadn't expected a mother, let alone this mother. What did this awful drunken woman reveal about Karen? Nothing at all, I told myself sternly, I couldn't judge people by their mothers. Or could I?

'This 'ere's a friend of your Karen,' one old man said at last, pointing at me.

'A friend of a friend,' I hurried to correct him. 'Someone I work with is a friend of hers.'

Jean made a kind of crowing sound. 'Didn't I tell you that bastard would come back for her?' she said.

I shook my head. 'I don't think . . .'

'Fat lot you know,' Jean said. 'That bastard, he doesn't deserve her, or the bairn; he thought she wasn't good enough for him, but he was the love of her life and even a pompous prick television star can't fight love.'

She laughed as she swallowed the rest of the whisky and

held the glass out for more.

It was grotesque, the raddled hag flirting with the ancient men, and it was only lunchtime.

The landlord poured Jean another drink. He winked at the old men. 'So, likely they'll be getting wed, your girl and her mystery TV star, eh Jean?' he said. The three men were laughing at her.

'He'll be making one of those TV celebrities out of you on his programme, like as not,' one old man said. They all laughed again.

Karen's mother pouted and gave the old man an arch look.

My God, I thought, she thinks she's Marilyn Monroe.

'Aye,' said the other old man, 'likely The Mother-in-Law From Hell.' He could scarcely get the words out, he was laughing so much.

Jean wasn't listening to him. 'There's no good comes of messing with my girl,' she said. 'I always said that. Didn't I always say that?'

The landlord grinned. 'More'n once, Jean,' he said.

'Happen young Andy Little'll have something to say about that,' one old man said.

'Andy Little!' Jean pretended to spit on the floor. 'Over my dead body,' she said.

'Fancy a crack at him yourself, do you, Jean?' the landlord asked.

He and the old men laughed again.

Jean laughed too. 'Why not?' she said. 'He's closer to my age than he is to hers. I was a child bride when I fell for Karen.'

They had all forgotten me. I slipped out of the pub into the raw grey afternoon.

A dour grey-haired woman waiting at the bus stop among a pile of shopping bags gave me directions to the Midgley house. I hadn't meant to ask where Karen lived, I'd meant to turn round and go back to Castleborough, where I was in control of what I was doing. Or, at least, I could put up a good show of pretending to be. In this God-forsaken hole I didn't seem to have any sort of control over my own actions.

I'd left my mobile phone on the driving seat. There were two messages from Simon. 'Ring me,' and, 'Why don't you ring me?'

I turned off the phone.

I'd drive past her house. There was no harm in that.

So I set off up a narrow lane and soon I couldn't have gone back if I'd wanted to. There was nowhere to turn the car. The tarmac road gave way to a metalled track, then rutted grass and slabs of bare rock. I could see buildings ahead which must be the Midgley farm. I'd turn the car in the yard and drive back the way I'd come.

The house seemed to grow out of the granite hillside. It was a two-storey cottage protected by farm buildings. There were a few bedraggled chickens in the yard. A group of scrawny sheep stood in a gateway. Otherwise, the place seemed deserted.

I turned the car and then hesitated before driving away. I felt guilty, as though I was about to read someone's secret diary.

Then I saw a young woman walking across the fell towards the farm. I knew at once that this was Karen, it had to be because there was a resemblance to the woman in the pub. In twenty years, I thought, she'd look exactly like that raddled tart. I liked the idea of that, but it wasn't really true. There was something innocent and untouched about the young woman coming across the fell. The woman in The Black Bull didn't have that and looked as though she never had.

Grudgingly, though, I felt sorry for Karen's mother. It

must have been hard to live with a constant reminder of her own youth. Karen looked about my age, or very little older. Long blonde hair streamed behind her like a pennant. She wore jeans and an anorak against the wind, all ordinary enough, but there was something about her that gave an overwhelming impression of warmth and corked vitality. She was carrying a wicker basket which she swung as she jumped gracefully from boulder to boulder down the hillside. I heard nothing, but she appeared to be singing at the top of her voice, her body moving to the unheard beat. It all looked like a scene from *The Sound of Music*. It was grotesque.

I put the car in gear and drove away slowly. I didn't look back to see if Karen Midgley saw me. I didn't want to catch another glimpse of her, I told myself it would be unlucky, like seeing a single magpie. Really I was afraid that another sight of that golden young woman would dent my resolve. Karen looked too uncomplicated to hate. But she was Simon's enemy and mine and I mustn't soften.

I remembered that she was an actress, or at least she'd worked in television; she'd seen a lot of actresses, of course she knew how to look innocent. But why did she bother out here, with only an audience of sheep and seagulls in this wild, deserted place? Ingrained deceit, that was why.

How dare she sing? How dare she skip down a mountain as though she hadn't a care in the world? She was triumphant. She was thinking of Simon and what she'd get out of ruining him. Money? Fame? Or just simple revenge? She'd have them all. And she was protected whatever lies she told. She was anonymous, shielded by law. Afterwards she'd make a fortune telling her victim story to the tabloids; everyone would pity her for what she said Simon had made her suffer. Another bloody victim. And, as the car bumped and bucked its way down the track, I was full of bitterness. I hated her. I'd seen her, so now I knew exactly who it was I hated, and I knew now it wouldn't be enough to make her suffer: I wanted her dead.

I was glad I'd gone to Brockbeck.

11

Learning to Hate the Enemy

Later, back home in Castleborough, I rang Simon.

'Where were you?' he asked. 'I tried all day to get you.' His voice was slurred.

He was drunk, I shouldn't have rung. Already he was looking for a fight.

'Busy,' I said, 'I turned off the mobile.'

'I wanted to talk to you.'

He sounded maudlin, accusing me.

'What did you want to tell me?'

It was like talking to a child and I'd never been good with children.

There was a pause.

'I'm not telling you,' he said, and put the phone down.

Thank God for that, I thought. Then I began to worry about whether I should ring back to check on him.

In bed, with the late-night sounds of the city outside the window making a mockery in my head of that desolate hillside and the grim grey village, I lay sleepless. It seemed to me that I'd stepped outside civilization that day into a primitive world where normal human standards not only did not apply, they were absurd. There it was natural I should hate Karen as I did, I didn't feel guilty about it like I did here in the city. There it seemed normal, but here in Castleborough I felt guilty.

But every time I closed my eyes, I saw that young woman swinging her basket and singing. I hadn't expected Karen to be like that. She'd seemed so . . . carefree was the only word I could think of. There was nothing about her at all to suggest that she'd been driven to accuse Simon by any kind of rational need. That fuelled my resentment.

At last I forced myself to admit it: I was jealous of that golden, glowing, young woman.

Marta Blane had said that Karen wasn't that good-looking, but she was wrong. Or perhaps, she was being nice and sparing my feelings. Anyway, I was certain now that Simon had been in love with Karen Midgley, and she with him. She'd had his child, for God's sake. What he and I had now couldn't compete with that, not even at its best it couldn't, and it never would. He'd never even been able to tell me about the child, not even when I'd suggested we had a baby together as a new beginning. I knew what that said about his relationship with me, but what did it say about his relationship with her?

'Oh, God,' I said aloud in the darkness, 'Karen Midgley thinks he belongs to her. This is her way of claiming him back.'

And, as I said this, I stopped feeling guilty about abominating Karen. I was learning to hate the enemy and it felt good.

12

The Corpse Still Dead

Simon's next court appearance was coming up. Now the police would have to declare if they intended to proceed to trial. The night before I'd argued with Simon on the phone. It had lasted most of the night. I wanted to be there, but he wouldn't have it.

'No,' he insisted, 'I don't want you to go through that. I want to come home to you when it's all over and then we'll have the rest of our lives together.'

'No, no,' I'd pleaded, 'I want to be there for you, I must be there whatever happens.'

'But don't you understand,' he said, 'I don't want to associate you with it? Please listen, Sara. This nightmare is nothing to do with us. You don't belong among these people. That's why I love you. I couldn't stand seeing you there. It's bad enough watching you read the bloody stories in the newspapers. Please, my darling, don't come.'

'But suppose . . .'

'Oh ye of little faith.'

He'd sounded like his old self then, making a joke of it. I fought back tears. 'I've no doubts about you; I know you didn't do it,' I said, 'but British justice is something else.'

'I love you,' he said. I heard the catch in his voice.

'Me, too,' I said. 'See you later.'

I could see his point. If he was found not guilty, he would be able to move on more easily if the sight of me at the breakfast-table didn't remind him of what had happened.

At lunchtime I took a sandwich into the sitting-room and turned on the television news before going to work.

Simon appeared on the screen.

He was being filmed on the steps of his apartment building. He was surrounded by a crush of people.

I thought it was old footage. The television people would have prepared a preview of the trial later that day. The morning news on television did this a lot, telling us what was going to happen rather than what was actually happening. It drove me mad, it was really bad journalism. I wanted to know what happened, not what some moron commentator thought might happen. And then when they guessed wrong, they never admitted it, they simply adjusted what did happen to suit their own misinformation.

Anyway, there was Simon on the screen. It was a rainy day and he wasn't wearing a raincoat. There were darker wet patches on his dark grey suit. A gusty wind whipped his damp blond hair across his face. He didn't seem to notice. He looked like someone suffering from shell shock. His expression was the same bland mask of bonhomie-in-a-hurry I'd seen so often when he was trying to reach his car through a crush of fans.

Then it dawned on me that what I was watching on TV was live.

I heard the reporter say, 'This is the scene today after police told disgraced TV celebrity Simon West that in the light of new evidence they have withdrawn all charges against him. The star, best known as the host of the hit show

Where There's Muck There's Brass, will appear in court later today for formal confirmation of this, but that's the latest from outside the star's home.'

The reporter joined the general rush forward towards Simon, shouting with the others.

A voice cried out, 'Simon, how do you feel?' Another yelled, 'What do you have to say now about British justice?'

Simon, expressionless, stopped before the bank of cameras. Beside him, a small, dark man in a beautifully cut pin-stripe suit stepped forward and started to speak. I recognized him. He was the flashy little man who'd witnessed that awful scene in the cocktail bar of The Grand Hotel. The caption on the TV screen read, 'Malachi Mahoney, spokesman for Simon West'. He began to read from a prepared script:

'My client has authorized me to make a statement. He is naturally very relieved that the police have decided not to pursue the allegations made against him. He has nothing to say about the possible motive for these allegations, but he is glad that he can now put what has been a nightmare behind him and concentrate on taking up his career without a stain on his character. He has always said that he looked forward to refuting the charges against him at his trial, and he is grateful that this has now been done.'

Mal stepped back.

Simon smiled.

What had happened? 'What new evidence?' I asked aloud.

'What about compensation?' someone in the crowd shouted. 'Are you going to sue the police?'

Someone else demanded, 'Are the police going to charge the woman involved?'

Mal was about to step forward to answer, but Simon stopped him.

'There's been enough unnecessary suffering over this,' he

said. 'I'm not looking for revenge. I want to draw a line under it and get on with my life. I hope that with all charges against me withdrawn, this will now be possible.'

As he spoke, I started to weep. He sounded so sad. If he hadn't known before, he'd know now that it was Karen, the mother of his child, who'd accused him, he must be terribly hurt. The tears flowed down my face. I'm happy, I told myself, I shouldn't be crying. It's over. And Karen Midgley was over, too. He couldn't possibly have any good feelings for her now.

Maybe I should have felt relief. I wanted to. But I felt disappointed. And frightened. This wasn't a solution, it wouldn't even start to put right the damage Karen Midgley had done. We could never get back to the way things had been before. It was like when a doctor pulls a sheet over a dead body, hiding the horror, but the corpse is still there dead. I told myself I was being stupid, it was over, everything would be all right.

I wondered what I should do? There was no point trying to contact Simon, he'd be busy for hours. Perhaps he'd ring me, but that would probably be difficult. He wouldn't be alone, he'd be afraid some reporter might overhear him.

I didn't need the details, anyway. Everyone knew now Simon didn't do anything wrong and a lot of people would have to eat their words.

I changed channels to see the next news bulletin. I saw Simon appear at the court to be told that the police were offering no evidence against him, that he left the court without a stain on his character. Newsreaders speculated about whether Simon West would be back on the screen presenting his popular prime-time game show next weekend.

Later, at work, I heard more details. Simon West's accuser had failed to turn up in court. She'd refused to go through with her evidence. That destroyed the police case. None of the other women who'd come forward had been able to offer any reliable evidence which would stand up in court. The prosecution had nothing else to go on. No, they were not going to pursue the woman for wasting police time. These cases were very sensitive, they said. In other words, Simon's anonymous accuser, whether raving lunatic, self-seeking drama queen, or spiteful bitch, would escape unscathed, never even be held to account for what she'd done.

Sure, I thought, that might be all right for the police, but what about Simon? Why didn't he want Karen punished? Did he still feel something for her? Was he thinking of what it might do to his kid if he pursued her? Why hadn't he told me about the child long ago? Would he tell me now, if I asked why he wasn't going to take action against Karen?

I tried to stop myself doing this, why couldn't I just be happy?

In the office there was a continuing flow of copy coming in from the agencies to be incorporated in the story. According to these reports, Simon's employers were considering his future. There were no immediate plans to reinstate him.

'But that's saying they think he's guilty anyway,' I protested to Frank. 'He left the court without a stain on his character. Are you sure the reporter's got it right?'

'They're saying that whether or not the police can prove he did it, he's still a sleazy little shit,' Fortuny said with the air of one who knows. She pursed her pale lips in an expression of righteous judgement and her colourless eyes peered over the rims of her spectacles so she reminded me of an old-fashioned school ma'am castigating cowed children. God, how I disliked her.

'There's no smoke without fire,' Fortuny said.

'He should sue,' I said.

'He's not going to, though, is he?' she sneered. 'You heard

that crap about not wanting revenge. He doesn't want any closer investigation, more like. You can't blame people thinking he's got away with it.' Fortuny sounded righteously indignant.

Frank said, 'You can't change the way people see it.'

'Why would that poor woman lie about being raped?' Fortuny asked. 'OK, so she didn't turn up in court, but that doesn't make him not guilty. Either he paid her off, or she couldn't face the publicity. Imagine how you'd feel, facing the sort of questions they ask rape victims in court.'

She sounded smug, like the official representative of virtuous, much-wronged womanhood.

I could feel myself go red. 'I know exactly how I feel now,' I snarled. 'That woman's a bitch and she should be punished for what she's done. But she won't be because she's never even been named. There's no come-back at all against her, she's totally protected. It's not fair.' I was shouting.

Fortuny laughed. 'You don't have to shout,' she said. 'Justice has been done, after all. The story's over now. That's an end to it.'

'Is it?' I said. I knew it wasn't. The corpse was still there dead.

13

Apocalypse Now

If only that had been the end of it, not just for Simon, but for me too.

I couldn't get rid of the fear that there was worse to come. Fortuny and her prejudices wouldn't be alone. That girl typified the great British public. To them, Simon wasn't innocent, simply he couldn't be proved guilty. They liked to kick celebrities when they were down, regardless of justification. I knew the score: I'd had it drummed into me for long enough, the first lesson of tabloid journalism: set 'em up and knock 'em down.

Intimations of the problems Simon faced from now on were clear from the first. For a start, there was the ominous refusal of his bosses to reinstate him immediately. In the face of direct questions from the media, the men in suits prevaricated. His slot had already been filled, they said, they would be looking for the right opening for him some time in the future.

And on a television debate on the very day of Simon's acquittal, the female producer of a prime-time family show said that her first priority must always be to protect young people from the sort of person who could get himself accused of a crime like rape.

'Even when he didn't do it?' I shouted at her big screen face. 'Can't you see what you're saying?'

I didn't want to believe it, but I heard that producer say it and I knew her view would be shared by so-called liberal people everywhere. Before the end of that very first day it was becoming obvious that, as Mal was no doubt trying to find a way of putting tactfully, 'The boy's too hot to handle.'

I was filled with foreboding as I drove home that night. What would this do to Simon? I longed to see him, and dreaded it at the same time. I was scared for him. And a little *of* him, of how he would react to this massive betrayal. I tried to pull myself together. We'd got each other. None of the other stuff mattered compared to that. Simon was officially innocent, he'd stop drinking and we'd get married and start again somewhere else.

I was so distracted by my fears, I almost ran into the car in front before I realized there was a traffic hold up.

A police car, blue light flashing, was slewed across the main road over the bridge into the city centre. A policeman was diverting the traffic.

Oh God, I thought, someone must've jumped off the bridge, poor sod.

As I passed the policeman I lowered the window and showed my press card.

'Someone jump off the bridge?' I asked him.

'No, I don't think it's that,' he said. He was very young and looked harassed. 'Something's up in the city centre. We've been told to close the bridge except for emergency vehicles, that's all I know. They don't tell us anything.'

As I followed the diverted traffic, I was thinking it was probably too early for a suicide, not midnight yet. People who threw themselves off the bridge usually did it in the small hours, when the streets were deserted. At this hour of the night there were still pedestrians about, as well as heavy through traffic. Anyway, whatever was happening, at least I was off duty. I'd been waiting a long time for this night with Simon, just him and me and the promise of a real future together. If something big had happened, it would mean front-page rewrites for the final edition. Fortuny would have to cope with it. Serve her right. But it was probably nothing more than the gas company dealing with an emergency leak near the shopping centre, which would let Fortuny off the hook. A traffic jam because of a gas leak rated only a few paragraphs. She'd probably rather have the suicide, at least she could act the queen bee, rewriting the front page and bossing the printers about.

It came to me then that something wonderful had just happened. For a moment there I was back to being a normal, ordinary sub reacting to a routine story. I'd forgotten about what had been happening to me and Simon. It made me start not just to hope but to believe that perhaps after all Simon and I could get through this and live a normal life.

I was relieved that whatever the traffic problem was, I wouldn't be much delayed getting home. Simon would be at his flat by now. He'd be waiting to ring me. I knew there wasn't much chance, even tonight, that he'd stay over at my place. The photographers would hang around to see him safe at home alone before they packed up for the night. Being hunted and taking cover had become a bit of a habit for him. Well, that would change soon.

But as I drove along Riverside Parkway close to the regenerated docks area, I couldn't altogether shake off my forebodings. I thought of calling in on Simon, braving the media. But he wouldn't want that. He'd be worn out and so was I.

At home he'd left a message on my answering machine. He

93

said, 'Love you. I'm bushed and going to bed now. Tomorrow we'll be together for good. Sleep well.'

I picked up the telephone, just to say goodnight. But he wouldn't thank me for waking him by ringing.

I went to bed.

I lay awake, desperate to sleep, but beset by fears about the future. What would happen if Simon couldn't get work?

I imagined the hours we'd spend trying to come to terms with his new, empty, lonely life. He'd keep drinking; I'd be all he had; he'd demand all my attention; he'd have to live through me. Nothing would change, it would be the same as the last few months. Could I cope with that?

As I lay in the dark, my feet freezing even under the duvet, fear and uncertainty mocked my chaotic doubts. What did love mean? I didn't know Simon except as a celebrity. He was used to adulation, excitement, admiration. How could I, dull and ordinary, young, fat, fierce me, make up to him for losing his career? Not without being consumed by his need for all those things. He'd be full of self-pity at first, of course he would, and I'd listen and be sympathetic, of course I would. But could I keep it up for weeks, months, years? And try as I might, I couldn't stop the voice in my head telling me over and over again that no, I couldn't, that in the end I'd want to escape the tyranny of his dependence on me.

My God, he'd been exonerated, I should've been over the moon. Would I rather he was in prison for something he didn't do? Or even, would it be easier if he'd done it, because that would set me free? I asked myself how I could even think such a thing, but I had thought it and I hated myself for it.

In the end I took a sleeping pill. I dreamed I was in a busy street trying to find Simon. I was frantic. People turned to stare at me as I pushed my way through the crowd. They all had Simon's face, but they were strangers.

The telephone woke me early next morning. I jumped up to answer it, sure it must be Simon. But it was Nigel from the office, the chief sub-editor on the day shift. I didn't recognize his voice at once, but then I scarcely knew him except by sight in the office. He wore glasses and his dark-brown hair looked as if it was painted on his head like a Dutch doll's, never a hair out of place. He was always on the point of going home when I came in, and I often thought I wouldn't want to work the early shift because there was something about him I didn't like.

'I've two subs off sick and all hell's breaking loose here,' he said. He sounded fraught. He added, 'You were on the first evening shift last night, weren't you? You're the only one I can ask to come in.'

I didn't mind. Even through the doped fug in my head, I was quite pleased. Working through the day, I'd have the night off. Simon and I could spend it alone, the first night of the rest of our life together.

It felt odd going into the office in the morning. The place seemed much more crowded than later, full of people I scarcely knew. I sat at the far end of the sub-editors' table, where there were several empty places.

Nigel, looking harassed but perfectly coiffed, came towards me with a sheaf of paper. 'Sara, thank God you're here. This lot all seem to be trainees and this story needs careful handling.'

'OK,' I said, 'what's it about?' I sounded too bracing because I was trying to counteract his fussiness.

'We've had all this copy in from the stringers,' Nigel said in his precise little voice, 'it'll need to be pulled together with what's in the computer as it comes in from our guys on the scene.'

He was talking as though it was my first day doing the job, and it irritated me.

I asked, 'God, Nigel, what on earth is this story? It sounds like the Apocalypse.'

Nigel pushed his fistful of loose pages into my hand.

He said, 'Oh, sorry, I thought you knew. Simon West took a dive off the multi-storey car park in the town centre last night. They've just identified him formally.'

14

Death by Prejudice

Everything swam in front of me. I dropped the sheets of paper. The noise of the office seemed to be coming from a great distance.

Then Nigel's voice reverberated in my skull: 'What on earth's got into you? For Christ's sake, Sara, pull yourself together. This is a big story. He's written us a letter. Exclusive. This puts us way ahead of the nationals.'

I heard myself whisper, 'Nigel, I can't.'

'Of course you can. You're the only sub I've got here who can. I'll even give you a byline with the reporters, how's that? But get on with it. I'm overdue at the editorial conference.'

He threw a handwritten page on the desk in front of me and was gone. The sheet of paper was covered in Simon's spiky scrawl.

I picked it up. My hands were trembling so much I couldn't read what Simon had written. I laid the letter flat on the desk. My eyes blurred. A tear spilled on to the paper and left a smudge where the ink ran.

I dropped to my knees under the table, picking up the sheets of copy I'd dropped. I couldn't let anyone see my face.

I'd break down if anyone asked what was wrong. I crouched on the floor and squeezed my eyes tight shut to keep back the tears.

In the end I took Simon's letter to the lavatory. I locked myself in a cubicle.

There I took several long shuddering breaths and then I started to read. The letter was addressed to the Editor.

By the time you read this, you'll know what I've done. I'm sending this letter to you and not to any other newspaper because in the early days of my career when I was on local television in Castleborough, you and your readers gave me a lot of support. So now I feel more betrayed by you than any of the others. I trusted you, and when you turned against me, I felt particularly hurt. You automatically assumed I was guilty. I've read the headlines in your first edition tonight about what happened in court today. Not a hint that you were all wrong about me; not a word of apology. You keep on about better being safe than sorry, about how the poor girl must have been under intolerable pressure, that she must be mentally sick. Not a word about what she's done to me. It's as though I don't exist as a person at all.

I've decided there's no point going on in a world where proving your innocence makes no difference to the way people treat you as guilty. I can't face living like that. So do me one last favour and don't let the coroner fudge the issue with some stupid verdict about the balance of my mind being disturbed. This is a case of death by prejudice; the murder weapon is the gutter press. You lot.

Simon had signed his name with a flourish.

I sat and stared at the letter. He must have driven to the office last night and left it at reception on his way to the multi-storey car-park.

And I was here, I was upstairs thinking of him. If he'd only come upstairs, I could've stopped him.

But of course he knew that, and he hadn't wanted me to stop him.

I felt sick and I was very cold. My teeth were chattering. Somewhere nearby someone was making a low moaning sound like keening. It was irritating. I flushed the lavatory to drown the noise but it didn't stop. Then I realized it was coming from me. Yet it seemed to have nothing to do with me. I couldn't stop it. I was the one who'd betrayed him. I'd failed him. Those thoughts I'd had, about the way things might have been, he'd known I'd feel like that. I'd never realized. I'd been selfish, thinking of myself, and of course it wouldn't have been that way anyway because Simon was Simon and he wasn't a coward, he was brave and funny and full of life and it wouldn't have happened.

Someone banged on the outer door of the Ladies. I heard Nigel shout my name. I folded Simon's letter carefully.

'Be with you in a second,' I shouted. Nigel muttered something about female priorities. I put the letter to my lips and said softly, 'I won't let you down, my love. I'll make sure she doesn't get away with this.'

I shouted to Nigel, 'I'm coming. Keep your hair on.'

As I opened the door, he looked at my face and said, 'Are you all right? I'm sorry, were you a fan or something?'

'No,' I said, 'something I ate. I'm perfectly all right.'

I felt like a Judas.

And I vowed as I walked back to my desk with Simon's letter in my hand, *You're going to pay for this, Karen Midgley, if it's the last thing I do.*

I was like a zombie, going through the familiar motions. The least I could do was ensure Simon got sympathetic coverage. Several times I was glad to be among virtual strangers, though. Someone like Fortuny would have noticed something odd about me and made some bitchy comment.

At the end of my shift, I drove home in a daze. There was a pile of letters and junk mail on the doormat. I picked them up and sorted them like an automaton.

I recognized Simon's handwriting at once.

There was an actual physical pain behind my ribs. Simon was dead. Until then, during the day at work, I'd managed to keep his actual death at bay. I'd forced myself to treat his suicide as impersonally as any other newspaper story. I even succeeded in dissociating myself from that bitter public suicide note. But this letter was for me alone.

I couldn't bring myself to do more than skim what he'd written to me, not at once. But still the words burned my eyes. *Sara, forgive me. I can't face it. I know you love me, but you don't know what it would be like. That incident with those women in The Grand cocktail bar was only a taster.*

I thought he'd forgotten that.

He wrote, *It couldn't last between us, but before I forced you to give up on me, you'd have lost everything you are and want to be. That's the Sara I love. This is the only way I know to give you a chance of being happy.*

And then the final paragraph, which I took in and then heard myself repeating aloud – *I feel I've betrayed you, because you believe that I was innocent. I can't believe that myself any more. That woman who accused me must believe I raped her. She must. She believes I did, and in the face of everything that's happened, now I can't even be sure I didn't. That's what I can't live with. Don't hate me for this, Sara. Forgive me if you can.*

I ripped the letter to shreds, then threw them on the floor and trampled on them.

I was beside myself with fury.

'Bastard,' I howled, 'bastard, drunken bastard.'

There was nothing rational about my anger. It seemed to me at the time that what he'd written was a betrayal of everything we'd gone through together, because he *was* innocent. He knew that as well as I did. And now, with his stupid paranoid doubts, he'd made a nonsense of everything we'd had together. He didn't even really have doubts, he knew they weren't real.

'Coward,' I fumed, 'you're a coward. You've left me alone with nothing to live for.'

I poured myself a drink, and then another. I didn't know what I was doing; what I was thinking, or feeling, even. I couldn't take it in that Simon was dead. I didn't believe it.

Then the anger erupted in a cataclysm of weeping which left me feeling weak and empty inside. Simon was dead; I'd better believe it.

He hadn't made his sacrificial gesture for me, he'd done it for her, for Karen. He cared enough for her to kill himself, but he didn't love me enough not to.

My self-pity wasn't very attractive, but I couldn't stop my emotional rampage. It really bugged me to have to admit I was savagely jealous of Karen. She had more of him than I did; he had a child with her, but he wouldn't with me. He'd loved her and he'd killed himself for what he thought she thought he'd done to her; not for me.

I tried to tell myself that nobody sane could think this way, but I did. It was driving me mad. And I was overwhelmed by guilt. Simon had written *before I forced you to give up on me*. I'd scarcely admitted to myself I'd ever had such thoughts of giving up, but I had. He'd known me better than I knew myself. I didn't know how to bear it that he'd known that I'd betrayed him in my head, if not in action.

I sat for hours dry-eyed in the dark, trying to make sense of how I felt. I reached no conscious conclusions; I made no actual decision, but as dawn broke behind the roofs of the blank-faced buildings across the road, I knew with a certainty which scared me that I wouldn't have any peace ever again until Karen Midgley had paid for what she'd done.

I saw her in my mind's eye, blonde hair flying in the wind, skin glowing, striding across that bleak northern hillside like a Norse goddess, happily singing. She'd no right to be alive like that.

I was going to make sure she wouldn't be alive like that for long.

15

To Kill a Mockingbird

In the days that followed, I found myself thinking more about Karen Midgley than about Simon himself. I wanted to think about him, to try to remember the good times and the many little things that had made us happy. But every time Simon came into my head, Karen Midgley followed and elbowed him out of the way. She was an almost tangible presence in every part of my home, the bathroom, the kitchen, and, most of all, the bedroom. Everything I did, I could feel Karen Midgley mocking me. She was everywhere except in the newspapers.

I scoured these every morning for Simon West's accuser's story. She wasn't likely to miss the chance to make money. She needed it. I'd seen how she lived in that dump of a broken-down farm in Brockbeck. She was obviously poor, of course she'd cash in. She'd do it for the child, if for nothing else.

I couldn't come to terms with Simon's death. I felt bereft, betrayed, guilty and angry, and rather than focus all these negatives on Simon, I blamed Karen Midgley.

It was hard to grieve when no one even knew I'd been

bereaved. All around me, all the time, people were talking about Simon, and all they said was sneering or judgemental. I'd never dreamed it could be so hard to have no one to talk to about what was happening to me. I felt horribly isolated. At one point I almost even called my mother. One night I got home from work and was so spooked by my empty house that I rang the office just to speak to another human being. If I'd got through to Frank then, I'd have told him everything. That's what I wanted. But Fortuny answered the phone. I hung up.

Two days after Simon's death, and a week before his funeral, I was driving up a side street near the office when I saw a funeral cortège at the entrance to a church.

Without really thinking what I was doing, I parked the car and followed the coffin inside.

I sat at the back, well away from the small group of mourners gathered at the front behind the altar rail.

This was how it should have been, this was how ordinary people grieved and came to terms with tragedy. And after this, they started to get back to normal.

I began to weep, and, having started, I couldn't stop. People turned to look at me.

Then an elderly woman got up from the pew where the close family sat and came up to me.

'What are you doing here?' she hissed. 'You should be ashamed coming here intruding on grief. Haven't you done enough harm to this family already, you and his other floozies?'

I was weeping so much, I couldn't speak. I saw the expression of contempt and distress on her face and I fled from the church.

I sat alone in the car in the now deserted street.

I kept whispering, 'I'm sorry', but I don't know who I thought I was apologizing to.

I don't know how long I sat there. I was late for work.
Frank would do his nut.

Things got a little easier as Simon's name disappeared
from the front pages. There was a subdued flurry of attention
with coverage of the coroner's verdict at the inquest – that
he took his own life while the balance of his mind was
disturbed. It was revealed, too, that he'd been drinking
heavily before he killed himself, but what didn't come out
was what had driven him to drink. Honestly, reading the
garbage written about him, I'd have thought he was a long-
time alcoholic if I hadn't known him.

The coroner's finding was inevitable, too. So much for
Simon's hopes of a verdict of death by prejudice. But the
inquest offered the newspapers a platform for yet more
features about the dangerous social and moral consequences
of celebrity.

I suppose none of the lies and nonsense should have
mattered to me any more. I could still cherish the Simon I'd
known. If everyone else believed what they read in the newspapers, at least I could keep the real Simon to myself.

Or I could if Karen Midgley didn't exist. As I said, I
couldn't think of Simon without Karen forcing her way to
the front of my mind; I was forced to share my own Simon
with her. And whether I liked it or not, and of course I
didn't, whatever lies Karen Midgley had told, whatever she'd
done, she had known the real Simon, and she'd known him
first. He'd been her Simon before he was mine.

I couldn't forgive her for that. I couldn't forget it. It made
what Karen did much worse as far as I was concerned. She
hadn't merely exploited Simon's celebrity; she'd destroyed
the real man.

On the day of his funeral, I decided to act. I started to
prepare my revenge.

'Where's the Simon West rape-victim's story?' I asked

Frank when I came in to work the evening shift. 'She's leaving it a bit late to cash in, isn't she?'

I wasn't quite sober. I'd spent most of the day in a pub overlooking the fashionable church where Simon's funeral service was to take place.

I'd been waiting for Karen Midgley to turn up. I'd watched the crush of photographers and reporters on the steps.

There was no family there to mourn. According to the papers, Simon had no relatives. He'd been abandoned by his teenage mother, been brought up in care. He didn't have friends. He had fans. He'd had fans, strictly past tense. They didn't turn up at his funeral.

He'd called Mal his friend, but that relationship couldn't be called friendship in any sense that I understood the word. Mal was a professional friend and that was it, in my view. At least he was there, though.

All I knew was that Simon had deliberately cut himself adrift from his past. It was shaming enough that I'd learned more about his background from the obituaries after his death than he'd ever told me himself.

I didn't even know what religion he was, or if he believed in God. Mal must have arranged this funeral and chosen to have it in the C of E.

Outside the church, behind the banks of television cameras, a small crowd of the curious waited in silence as the coffin was taken inside. There were no friends, no celebrity colleagues, no lovers. Only Mal dressed up like an Irish bookie. He alone followed the undertaker's men into the church.

Thank God I hadn't gone to the service, the media vultures would've gone to town on the lone mystery woman who came to say goodbye to him. They'd probably even have had me down as the guilt-ridden phoney rape victim there to see the monster buried and preparing to dance on his grave.

But I wanted to be there, wished I could claim the right to mourn my lost love, take a first step in getting back to being normal.

But it was too late. If I came forward now as his fiancée, I'd look like some kind of hanger-on looking for publicity. Simon had wanted to protect me from all that, and he had. I must learn to live the life he'd dealt me.

So I had a few drinks and then a few more and then I was asking Frank about the lying bitch who'd brought the charge, which I knew was dangerous and provocative to mention, particularly in the state I was in. Frank didn't do broken hearts and feminine sentimentality.

'Why are you asking?' he said. He always wanted to know why.

'Professional interest,' I said, pretending detachment. 'Only, I'd have expected someone to track her down by now. If he was innocent, she must've done it for money.'

'It's a big if, though, isn't it?' Frank said.

'I don't know how you can say that after what's happened,' I said. 'That's the kind of attitude that drove him to kill himself.'

'If you ask me, suicide is the trademark of the guilty,' he said.

I ignored this. 'It'd be a good story,' I said. 'As one pro to another, admit you'd like to get hold of her.'

Frank laughed. 'One pro to another,' he said, 'Ted tried. She threatened him with a pitchfork if he went near her again. She's a countrywoman, apparently the pitchfork is her weapon of choice. Then she said she'd sue if he kept harassing her.'

That sounded like Karen Midgley. She looked like a bully to me. Being a manipulative victim is often the flip side of the bully. That woman looked far too sure of herself swaggering across her blighted hillside.

107

I thought about that for a bit. I knew I was kidding myself. Karen Midgley didn't look like a bully at all. That was one of the reasons it was so hard to come to terms with what she'd done. I couldn't reconcile the woman I'd seen with the person who'd falsely accused Simon.

I said to Frank, 'You should use a woman.'

'You offering?' Frank said, with a comical grimace full of cliché innuendo.

I smiled politely. It paid to smile at Frank's jokes.

'Wait and see,' I said, and hoped he didn't notice how I slurred the words. 'I might have something in mind.'

16

Making Holiday Plans

I said that to Frank out of bravado. But then, after a night of drunken unconsciousness – the first real sleep I'd had in what felt like years – I woke to find it true. I had a definite plan about my next step in destroying Karen Midgley.

I waylaid Ted of the wild boar eyes in the office. He reeked of aftershave and wore a less rumpled suit than usual, his shirt was almost clean, although, as always, the buttons struggled to contain his beer gut. Ted had done well out of the Simon West story. He now had the title chief crime reporter, and a guaranteed byline. He'd taken to violently flashy ties as a badge of office.

'I need your expertise,' I said, in my best wheedling voice. I reckoned that because Ted was ugly, he was even more susceptible to flattery than most men.

'As a reporter?' he said. 'Or are you about to commit a crime you want to get away with?'

It disconcerted me for a moment that he should think of crime in connection with me. What made him say that, my plans were my secret?

But, of course, he was joking. He laughed at my expression.

'If you're embarking on a life of crime, I'd cultivate a poker face before I started, if I were you,' he said.

'Good point,' I said, 'but I'm not cut out for it. It's nothing like that.'

'Shoot, then. I'm on my way out. I'm meeting the chief constable for a drink.'

What a prat he was. I was about to make some mocking comment, but instead I took a deep breath and smiled an ingratiating smile. I didn't want to alienate him.

'I'm writing a book about Simon West,' I said. 'I hoped you'd give me some background.'

His face changed at the magic word book. 'That's my story,' he said. 'Why should anyone ask you to write a book about him? You're a sub.'

Yes, I thought, it's my job to rewrite your copy so you don't look completely illiterate. But I knew the greedy defensiveness of professional jealousy when I saw it.

'No one has asked me to write it,' I said hastily. 'It's all my own idea. I don't want to be a sub for ever, you know. And it's the woman's angle I want to explore. You wouldn't be interested in that.'

Ted had had time to mask his resentment. He became patronizing.

'Can't see a publisher going for that myself,' he said. 'It's the sort of thing they'd get an old girlfriend to write, don't you think? Someone like Marta Blane, with a name people recognize.'

'She'd be too close to it, don't you think? I'm interested in what women saw in him, that sort of thing. You know, how wealth and celebrity make quite ordinary men attractive. That's where I thought you could help me. I want to talk to some of his old girlfriends. I thought you could put me in touch with the Midgley woman.'

'Her? She won't be any help,' Ted said. It was plain that the memory of the pitchfork incident made him angry. 'She's no use at all. Sick in the head, if you ask me.' He paused and gave me a hard look. 'Where did you get her name, anyway?'

'From the horse's mouth, Ted. You told me yourself.'

'Well, forget it. Try Marta Blane, she used to know your man pretty well.'

He walked away. I knew there'd be no more help from him. I wondered what had really happened between him and Karen, and what he'd said to make her attack him with the pitchfork. He'd probably tried it on and she'd turned him down flat. Men like Ted don't take kindly to being rejected.

Next I went to see Malachi Mahoney.

I wasn't sure what I hoped to gain from talking to Mal, but he'd been Simon's agent and closest friend, if a business arrangement can be described as friendship.

I suppose I wanted to know he felt the same way I did about what had happened to Simon. I didn't want him to *do* anything, I just wanted to talk about Simon with someone he'd been close to. I thought it would help me clarify my feelings.

I couldn't admit that what I really wanted was for Mal to confirm that my thirst for revenge against the woman who'd caused Simon's death was normal, reasonable even. I don't know how I expected him to do this, so perhaps what I really wanted was for him to comfort me and tell me to get over Simon and move on. I don't know, but I went to see Mal anyway.

His office was on the top floor of one of the few terraces of old riverside houses which hadn't been gentrified. As I climbed the stairs, it crossed my mind that Mal's business must have been badly damaged by the loss of its most high-profile client. True, the walls were lined with signed studio portraits of numerous handsome young men and glamorous women, but I recognized hardly any of them.

Mal was leaning across his secretary's desk as I walked into the office. He jumped away from the girl as though I'd interrupted something personal I wasn't supposed to see.

The little man looked less dapper than when I'd seen him with Simon in the cocktail bar of The Grand Hotel, or on television after Simon was exonerated without a stain on his character. He was in his shirtsleeves, with bright red armbands not altogether successfully holding back the cuffs above his plump hands. The pin-striped trousers of the suit he'd worn on both occasions now looked as if they could do with a press.

'I'm Sara Soames,' I said.

'Who?' Mal said, backing away towards a door leading out of the room. 'I'm afraid I'm not seeing clients today.'

'Mal, it's me, Simon West's girlfriend,' I said, and it was the first time I'd ever confessed to being Simon's girl in front of a stranger. The secretary didn't seem to take it in. 'We've talked on the phone,' I added.

'Oh, yes,' he said, 'poor Simon West. I'm sorry for your loss, love, but I'm afraid there's nothing owing to him, if that's what you're here to find out. In fact, even after the apartment's sold, I probably won't see a fraction of what he owed me.'

Mal's attitude was like a kick in the stomach. I couldn't hide my indignation. 'Of course that's not what I'm here for,' I said. 'I wanted to talk to you about him.'

He didn't try to pretend he wasn't relieved. But after all, he was a businessman, and there wasn't room for sentiment in business. I envied him a little, that he'd so clearly recovered from Simon's death.

'You were his closest friend,' I said. 'He said you were like a father to him.'

The secretary laughed.

'Poor Simon,' Mal said, 'the boy was sentimental; he always wanted people to like him.'

The secretary laughed again. Mal scowled at her and then he gave me a rather arch look which I took to be his way of deflecting any impression of cynicism.

'What's wrong with that?' I said. 'He thought you loved him.'

Mal heard the reproach in my voice. 'But of course I did,' he said. 'The money he earned, he was easy to love, isn't that right?'

'I loved him,' I said. I wanted to thump him, but I was afraid I was going to start crying.

'Of course you did, love. Me, too. But life goes on.'

The secretary suddenly blurted out, 'Another day, another dollar. Isn't that right, Mal?'

Mal looked at her, startled. Then he turned back to me.

'Try to look at it that he chose the right time to do what he did,' he said. He was obviously trying to sound sympathetic. 'Simon was a big star but he hadn't a cat in hell's chance of working again. Work was what he lived for. He could never have been happy without it, however hard he tried. Aren't I right, honey?' he said to the secretary.

'Who are we talking about?' the secretary asked.

'Simon West, for Christ's sake, who do you think?'

'The guy who killed himself?' the secretary asked.

'Forget it,' Mal said to her.

I went out. I didn't say goodbye.

Later, at work, I cornered Frank. 'You know what we were saying about the Simon West rape-victim story?' I said.

'What about it?' He was busy.

'If it's all right with you, I'm taking a month's holiday to work on it,' I said.

'What are you talking about now?' he said. 'Simon West is

dead in the water, kaput.'

'I'm owed the time off,' I said. 'It's none of your business what I do with my holiday.'

For the first time Frank turned to look at me.

'What do you have in mind?'

'I'm going to rent a place in the village where the woman who accused him lives, spend some time there. I'll think of a cover story.'

'She won't talk to you,' Frank said.

'She doesn't have to know she is,' I said. I sat down on an empty chair beside him. 'As far as she's concerned, I won't know who she is. She had anonymity hadn't she? But she must've had a relationship with him to accuse him, so some people in the village must know about the man. She won't know I'm there because of the rape charge. She won't have any idea I know she was the one who accused him.'

I was sounding too eager. Frank gave me a hard look and asked, 'How do you know this girl you're after is the one? No one's used her name.'

'Oh, Ted told me. Ages ago.'

'He should've kept his big mouth shut. That's how million-pound damage suits start.'

'Don't worry, I won't tell anyone. If she doesn't come across, no one's going to be any the wiser.'

Frank had lost interest. 'You're wasting your time, but you're due the time off,' he said. 'If that's how you want to spend your holidays, it's nothing to do with me. Put it on the roster.'

I got up to go and he said, 'And Sara, while you're at it, get a life.'

17

A Cold Welcome in Hell

I drove to Brockbeck the next day in heavy rain which was
turning to sleet.

The village looked no more welcoming than it had the last
time I was there. It was as though the place had been
attacked by some deadly chemical weapon. There was no
sign of human, nor even animal, life. The few trees were leaf-
less, their bark soaked black as coal by the rain. Although it
was only mid-afternoon, it was almost dark. I thought of the
streets of Castleborough, the shops full of light, the pave-
ments crowded with busy people, everyone and everything
full of life, and I wished I hadn't come.

Of course the Brockbeck people must be full of life, too;
they wouldn't survive in this churlish landscape if they
weren't. But as far as I could see they lived it in secret.
Brockbeck wasn't like Castleborough, where complete
strangers were accepted just because they were there. In a
sense, everyone in the city was a stranger to everyone else.
Here, the community seemed to put up barricades against
outsiders as though any visitor might carry plague. The way

I felt at that minute, it could've been true. And I hoped I'd pass it on.

I walked into the bar of The Black Bull. I remembered the landlord from my previous visit, a bulbous, balding man tending to fat. He was sorting his stock of mixers in a cupboard under the counter when I came in, and I was aware of his heavy breathing as he stood up to attend to me. He showed no sign of recognizing me.

'Yes?' he said, looking up as though I'd interrupted him at a busy moment.

'Do you have rooms?' I asked.

'What kind of rooms? There are all sorts of rooms, func-tion-rooms, games-rooms, meeting-rooms, but none of them are here.'

The landlord looked pleased about this roomless state. He seemed to take some sort of moral satisfaction in throwing cold water on people's unreasonable demands for rooms. He had a soft, sing-song accent I found hard to understand. I smiled to be polite.

'Bed and breakfast,' I said. 'I want to stay in the area for a while.'

I watched his face as avarice grappled with sloth.

'It's late for visitors,' he said. 'Minimum stay's a week this time of year. Short stays aren't economical, not with the work involved.'

'A week's fine. I'm doing some research into someone who used to have connections here. Simon West.'

'Never heard of him.' The landlord plainly wished he'd stipulated a longer stay.

'He was on television.'

'Never see it.'

At that moment the landlord's wife came in. He asked her, 'You ever heard of someone called Simon West, Doreen?'

Doreen, a stringy, hard-faced little woman, looked worried.

'I know the name,' she said. 'Is he a politician?'

'This young lady's come here to find out about him. She wants a room. She'll take it for a week.'

Doreen frowned and asked him, 'Why's she come here for something like that?'

She turned to me. 'There's not much call from tourists out of season. There's the one room you could have. You can pay the week in advance, or I'll need a deposit.'

I paid for the room in advance and followed Doreen upstairs.

It was a dull room, and cold. Magnolia paint, a yellow candlewick bedspread on a prim single bed, and net curtains at the window. I drew these back and sat on the edge of the bed looking out on the village street with the Methodist chapel opposite. I stared out through the sleety rain at the grey stone buildings and wondered what I thought I was doing here. I felt even more lonely than I had in Castleborough. This place was mean and ugly and looked dreary and desolate in the glow of the single subdued street lamp.

Here I was, though, so what did I do now? It was as cold inside the bedroom as it looked outside.

I almost grabbed my unpacked overnight bag and made a run for it. To hell with Karen Midgley, I wanted to be home in Castleborough with the heating full on and a good video to watch.

But I'd got a job to do. I felt I'd got a sort of commission from Simon to take vengeance on Karen Midgley, otherwise I really would go mad.

I went downstairs to the bar in search of warmth. It was still early in the evening, but surprisingly the bar was crowded. So there were real people living in this benighted place, and this was where they came after dark. I hadn't thought of this bleak bar as a focus of social life in this blighted village, but it probably saved these tight-fisted yokels the expense of lighting the fires in their own front rooms.

Christ, what a pack of hicks!

A group of loud young men who looked as though they might have come on from rugby practice were drinking beer; a couple at one table were snogging, and sundry old men played cards at another. One woman did demand attention. She was a bleached blonde siren past her prime who sat on a stool at one end of the bar trying to be flirtatious with the young rugby men.

I watched her and I could see she probably used to be good-looking. Now she wasn't she obviously couldn't break the flirting habit.

She looked familiar, or was she simply a pathetic female stereotype found in every pub anywhere?

Then she laughed and I recognized her - she was Karen Midgley's mother, Jean. I'd seen her before, in this very bar.

I had an odd feeling of déjà vu. The woman was clearly drunk. She kept slipping off the stool, almost knocking her chin on the counter before one of the rugby players caught her and pushed her roughly back into place. The young men all laughed uproariously every time this happened.

I took my drink to a table away from the bar. I wanted to study Karen's mother without being noticed.

Then a group of newcomers crowded the room. Soon a middle-aged couple sat themselves at my table.

I caught the woman's eye and smiled at her. She flushed and dropped her eyes.

There was a shout of laughter from the crowd at the bar. This time the rugby player had failed to catch Karen's mother as she slipped off her stool. She dropped slowly to the floor, her skirt rucked up to expose a black suspendered thigh.

The landlord was on the scene at once. 'Get her out of here,' he said.

'Nowt to do wi'us, John,' one of the young men protested.

He, too, spoke with the dying falls of the local accent.

I thought how hard it must be to have a real bloodletting shouting row up here, they all sounded as though they were singing everything they said.

His friend pushed the landlord aside. 'I'll take her home,' he said. 'John, help me get her into the back of the pickup.'

The landlord and another of the young men helped him haul Jean Midgley to her feet. They manhandled her out of the bar. As the door closed behind them, the young men cheered.

'Oh dear,' said the man at my table.

'Not again,' said the woman.

'What's that all about?' I asked.

The woman seemed to decide that some kind of apology to me as a stranger on behalf of the community was necessary.

'She's getting to be a public disgrace,' said the woman.

'Who is she?' I asked.

'Lives across the fell,' said the man. 'Lonely life, it must be.'

'It's the daughter I'm sorry for,' said the woman. She obviously resented her husband's effort to offer the drunken Jean Midgley any excuse.

'A daughter?' I said. 'She must be grown up, though. Why does she stay at home and put up with it?'

'She doesn't have much choice, poor girl,' the woman said. Her caressing tone reproached me for my hard heart.

'She's got guts, that Karen, I'll give her that,' the man said. 'Tries to scrape a living from that farm, and no help from anyone.'

The husband's sympathy for Karen turned his wife against her again.

'She'd have all the help she wanted if she got together with Andy Little like he keeps asking her,' she said. She curled her scarlet lip. 'Thinks she's too good for him, I suppose.'

'Give over, Betty,' the husband said. 'He takes that witch of a mother of hers home every time she keels over in here. I hope he's getting something for his trouble when he gets there. Karen's a lovely girl to look at, sure enough.'

'You can keep a clean tongue in your head, Daniel Carter,' said his wife.

She gave me a prim smile and then changed her tune about Karen Midgley.

'Karen's a nice girl, really,' she said, 'but she was once used to better things and we're not allowed to forget it. There's the little boy, too. It can't be easy for her with the child up in that wild place, not with her mother the way she is. Not much of a life to show for all her good looks.'

'Jean was a looker too,' Daniel said.

'In a cheap, tarty way she was,' Betty said, 'but that's what men go for, isn't it?'

I wasn't sure if that was a question for me or Daniel, but Daniel tried to change the subject. He said, 'And where's that boy's father, that's what I'd like to know. He should be helping out.'

'Go and get us another drink, dear,' Betty said.

Daniel stood up and collected the glasses. When he'd gone, I said to Betty, 'You said the daughter was used to better things? What happened to her?'

'Well,' said Betty, lowering her voice as though she might be overheard, 'she had a good job in TV in Leeds. She was in love with a man there, but he went off to be a big star and left her behind. They say he's the one left her pregnant with the little boy, but I don't know. It's years ago now.'

'That's sad, isn't it?' I said. 'Do you know who he was, the father?'

Betty shook her head. 'I don't know the names of any of those people,' she said. 'But he did Karen a bad turn, forcing her to come back here. She had to come back, you see, she didn't have anywhere else to go. She had to come back to her mother.'

I didn't necessarily see the logic of this, but I didn't want to argue the point with Betty.

I said, 'I suppose having that mother around wouldn't make it easy for a boyfriend who wanted to be famous. But the mother can't be much over fifty, surely?'

Betty Carter looked surprised at the question.

'She's fifty-one. I was at school with her,' she said. 'Of course she was a year or two ahead of me, but that's how old she is. You wouldn't think it to look at her now, but she was really good-looking once. She's ravaged by the drink now, of course, but if you saw her sober you wouldn't recognize her.'

Betty sighed and added, 'Poor Karen, having to put up with that.'

I didn't like the way Karen always seemed an object of pity.

'But when Karen came home Jean wasn't as bad as she is now,' Betty said. 'I suppose she didn't like the competition of a young, beautiful daughter around the place.'

Daniel came back to the table, carrying three full glasses.

'Here,' Betty said, 'I'll take them. You'll spill them.' She set down the drinks one by one and said, 'I was telling our friend here—'

'Sara,' I said.

'I was telling Sara, Dan, how Jean Midgley never had much of a drink problem before Karen came home to live here. Isn't that right?'

'Karen and the boy,' he said. 'Isn't that enough to turn anyone to drink?' He winked at me.

Betty clicked her tongue in mock protest. 'The kid's a nice boy, Dan,' she said, 'he wouldn't drive anyone to drink. Karen can be proud of Jack, the way she's brought him up.'

I choked on my drink. That was Simon's son she was talking about. The child hadn't seemed real to me until then, Simon's son, not a real person. But when Betty talked about him like that, he suddenly came to life in his own right. It was a shock, and it threw me. I'd got to get out of there before I did something silly and gave myself away. I choked and waved my hands in mute apology to Daniel and Betty, hoping they'd think I'd swallowed the wrong way, but it didn't matter what they thought. I had to get away from them. I had to be alone. I was overwhelmed with jealousy of Karen Midgley. Poor Karen, suffering Karen, with her drunken mother and her unproductive farm and the beefy rugby-playing boyfriend who wasn't good enough for her: Karen, the beautiful girl Simon had loved so much more than he'd loved me that he'd given her a son.

In my bedroom, with my head buried in the pillow, I almost wept tears of self-pity. I hated Karen Midgley. I couldn't bear it how much I hated her and I couldn't help the treacherous thought – was it Karen I hated so much, or was it Simon?

18

The Child

I was woken by the sound of children's voices. I pulled back the curtain and peered out of the window. It was still dark outside and I couldn't see my watch to tell what time it was in the feeble glow of the street light opposite. I did see a bunch of schoolchildren waiting around it, though. Then the school bus arrived and I watched the children get on.

One of them must surely be Jack, Karen's son and Simon's. I tried to guess which he was as the kids passed down the brightly lit bus, but the little boys all looked much the same to me. I've never had much to do with children, and I find it hard to tell them apart.

At breakfast, I asked the landlord and his wife – John and Doreen, they'd asked me to call them – about Karen and her son.

'Someone mentioned a television celebrity,' I said, 'was he the boy's father?'

'If you ask me,' Doreen said, 'I don't think he existed. I think she got herself into trouble and came back here with

123

that rigmarole about her celebrity boyfriend because it made her feel better about the shame of getting caught.'

'Now, Dor, that's not fair and you know it. It was Jean who invented the story about the TV celebrity.'

'But didn't Jack's father ever come here to visit?' I asked.

Doreen looked blank again. 'Him come here? Oh, no. No one saw hide nor hair of him. She knew him in Leeds when she worked there, and that's a fair step from here. Mind you, we hadn't seen hide nor hair of Karen before she came back when she got herself in trouble. She'd upped and gone as soon as she left school.'

'Aye,' said John, 'Jean's had a tough time of it over the years.'

'She's making up for it now, drunk every night of the week and you letting her get away with it,' Doreen said.

Why did married couples bicker and snipe at each other? Simon and I wouldn't have been like that. We wouldn't have bored one another; that was when it happened, when people got bored with each other.

I asked, 'Was Karen's father still alive? When she left home?'

'Karen's da?' Doreen laughed. 'If you ask me, Karen's da was one of those figments of Jean's imaginings. Like mother, like daughter. No one round here remembers no father.'

'Poor old Jean,' John said. 'She'd be in the bar here every night telling us all about Karen and how well she was doing. She's the one told us about Jack's father being a star on the television.'

'She never stopped talking about that girl of hers,' Doreen said, 'always on about the celebrities Karen knew and the parties she went to. She told us Karen and her TV star were engaged, but I don't know about that.'

'And then Karen got herself pregnant and came home?'

John said, 'Jean never mentioned the celebrity father after that.'

'Nor did Karen, not a word, so there's an end to it,' Doreen said.

Doreen gave me a sideways look.

'You know Karen, do you?' she asked. 'Asking about the boy and that? She's a friend of yours, is she?'

'You'll have known her in Leeds, is that right?' John said.

I wanted to change the subject. There was something about that crooning local accent that might lull me into saying too much. I got up to go.

'No, I don't know her myself,' I said. 'A friend of mine from the office asked me to look her up.' Doreen looked a bit doubtful, I thought. 'He used to work in television,' I added. 'I expect he met her there.'

I expect he did, I told myself. But I didn't know. I knew nothing about something that could've been the biggest thing in Simon's life. He'd never even mentioned her.

OK, so he'd left her when she was pregnant, which was bad, but they'd obviously been together. He'd probably offered to pay for an abortion, and when she wouldn't . . .

In my head I could hear Simon's voice repeating, 'We can't make it public that we're together yet. You know the fans need to think I'm single.' He'd said it to me, he'd have said the same thing to Karen when she told him she was pregnant. . . . 'It's the wrong time. Once I've made it, we'll be secure . . . then we can be a proper family.'

It suddenly seemed very important for me to see Jack. If he looked like Simon . . .

So that afternoon I was sitting in my parked car close to the dropping off point for the school bus. It was cold, wet and windy. I wanted to be inconspicuous, but I wasn't. There were several other cars waiting, but mine looked different. It was much too clean for one thing, and at least five years

125

newer than any of the others.

People noticed me. I didn't know what I'd say if someone asked what I was doing there. That was all I needed, one of these mothers thinking I was planning to abduct a kid. Why did it seem so important for me to see Jack? What difference was it going to make?

The school bus arrived. There was a flurry as the children jumped out to be grabbed by their mothers and hurried into the old cars. Then they were gone. Left behind, one small boy pulled up his collar and began to walk up the road towards the fell.

The child could've been about ten years old. I'd no idea how children looked at different ages. This kid was more than five or six and certainly not yet a teenager.

He was blond, like Simon. Like Karen, too, of course. He was thin, his scrawny knees shiny red with cold. He was growing out of his shorts, and the sleeves of his brown school blazer scarcely reached his wrists. I watched him scurry up the street, hunched against the wind.

Then I saw Karen. She was running down the road towards the child. Suddenly it was as though the cold, the wind and rain, had disappeared. The boy waved, beginning to race towards her. He threw his arms around her waist, looking up into her face, laughing. She was laughing, too, hugging him. Then they set off walking up the track, hand in hand, looking tremendously happy as though they hadn't a care in the world now they were together.

I felt sick. It was as though I was seeing Simon as a child, going home with his mother, except he hadn't had a mother; anyway, Simon before he knew the terrors of what would happen to him. I saw Simon, and I saw Simon's son, the son who should have been mine. And between them and me there was Karen Midgley.

126

My knuckles gleamed white as I gripped the steering wheel.

There was no choice, I couldn't help what was going to happen. It was her or me. I couldn't stop now.

19

Possessed

I'd been afraid in my life before, of all sorts of things. There'd been bullies at school. And I remembered how angry my father had been when he caught me stealing sweets from the village post office; I'd been afraid then. Years later, when I bought my house in Castleborough on a mortgage, there was the fear of being in debt, and always I was frightened of being fired from my job and losing the house.

I'd felt a kind of fear too when I met Simon and fell in love with him, about whether he would love me back; about losing him; about a future which should have been certain and was hopelessly vague. But it was wrong to call that fear, it was more like the kind of excitement which makes one nervous.

What I was feeling now was worse than any variation of fear I'd felt before. Horribly, I was afraid of myself. I no longer had control over my own actions.

I kept telling myself that I'd got to accept Simon was gone and move on. I must force myself to find a way to live the rest of my life without him. That was scary, but it wasn't what made me feel the way I did then.

Some implacable person inside me had already decided to act; I – the normal, ordinary person I recognized as myself – was afraid of what that action would be. It must be what people – or, at least, psychologists and poets – meant when they talked about the divided self. It seemed to me that my brain had lost touch with my emotions.

Oh, please God, I thought, don't let me be going crazy.

The bar at The Black Bull was empty. I could hear John's voice from the cellar, swearing over whatever he was doing. I hurried through to the stairs, not wanting to talk to anyone, most of all not to John. I found his obvious lack of enthusiasm for his own life depressing.

In my room I sat on the bed to try to sort things out. I looked out of the window at the empty street and the run-down shop and the frowning grey façade of the Methodist chapel and my mind echoed the same colourless blankness. I couldn't think.

At last, in an effort to pull myself together, I went down to the bar. I didn't want to talk, I wanted simply to sit undisturbed and watch other people being normal.

I'd settled at a quiet table before I recognized Karen Midgley and a young man sitting nearby. I'd seen the young man in the pub before. He was the stocky rugby player who'd taken Jean Midgley home one night. Andy something. Yes, Andy Little, I remembered that the name didn't fit him. He was anything but little.

He and Karen faced each other across the table. They were deep in an intense conversation which excluded everyone around them.

I studied them unnoticed. I heard Karen say Jack's name several times. It seemed to me that Andy Little didn't want to hear what Karen was telling him. He sat looking at the half-empty glass in front of him, not once raising his eyes to look at her face. He kept flexing his big red hands as though he was only just stopping them from strangling someone.

But Karen obviously wanted to get something off her chest and she wasn't going to stop now.

'So you see,' she said, 'I had to tell you. You've a right to know. There's no point in hiding the truth now.'

I knew she must be telling him about her and Simon, that Simon was Jack's father. She must've decided that Andy Little was a better bet for financial support than selling her story to the newspapers.

But Andy was shaking his head.

'Why now?' he said. 'Why did you wait so long to tell me about him?'

Poor sucker, he didn't realize the manipulative bitch had to be desperate to take him; he didn't at all compare with Simon.

I dismissed the thought that Simon wasn't in my life, either, any more, and I didn't even have an Andy Little to take his place.

What was I going to do with myself? There never would be anyone to take Simon's place for me. Was that worse than being Andy Little, some sort of second best? Had I been Simon's second best after Karen? I looked at the two of them, scheming Karen so sincere-seeming, Andy so plainly out of his depth. I felt sorry for him. Leave her, my thought waves urged him, but he only shook his head in a puzzled way and repeated his question.

'Why did you wait so long?'

Karen looked as though she didn't know what to say.

When she replied, she spoke very slowly.

'I felt guilty at first,' she said. 'I know, I didn't have to, but I did. It was only later I began to resent what he did. That was because of Jack, not for what he did to me.'

'But I don't see why you couldn't tell me. I knew you must've loved someone else, because you had Jack. We all come with emotional baggage. But I suppose I thought it was all dead and buried.'

It struck me as odd, hearing someone like Andy Little speak of *emotional baggage*. He seemed too big and macho to bother with New Man-speak like that.

But Andy still didn't look Karen in the face.

Karen said, 'I wanted to tell you, but in the end, I always chickened out. And suddenly one day it all seemed so pointless, living in the past. I saw that I was the one getting hurt, not him. It was up to me to stop it, so I did. That's why I'm telling you now, because I've put it all behind me.'

Andy Little stared at his big knotted hands.

'Does Jack look like . . . his father?' he asked.

He sounded pathetic, like someone waiting to be hurt.

'Not really. Don't you think he takes after me?'

Low-down lying bitch, he looks like Simon, just like Simon.

'Where's Jack now?' Andy Little asked.

He still spoke in that victim voice that, like his name, didn't suit him.

Karen said, 'He's staying over with a friend from school for the week. It's good for him to be part of a real family. And I needed to talk to you. I had to tell you, Andy. If there's any chance of you and me ever being together, you had to know the truth.'

'I'll get us another drink,' Andy said.

'No,' Karen said, 'this one will do me.'

She put her thin brown hand over his big fist.

She had beautiful hands, not like a farm labourer's.

'It was all over a long time ago, Andy,' Karen said. 'I've put the past behind me at last. A lot of things have changed for me now. I wanted to lay that part of my life to rest. I wanted you to know everything. Now I've told you. Let's get out of here.'

They got up to go. Andy pushed back his chair and caught my foot. He turned to apologize, but I knew he didn't even really see me. He looked shell-shocked.

I don't even know when I left the bar myself and went upstairs. I sat on the bed staring out at the raindrops falling like spent fireworks under the street light.

All I could think about was Simon dead and Karen Midgley preparing for a normal, ordinary, happy, married life.

And I knew exactly what it feels like to be possessed by a demon.

20

She's Driving me Crazy

I'd heard Karen tell Andy Little that Jack was away for the week. I hadn't expected to be in Brockbeck that long. But I wanted to see the boy again, if only as living confirmation that Simon had actually existed.

It wasn't easy to admit to myself, even, that I needed any such proof. But for some reason the Simon I knew and loved as a real person seemed to be slipping away from me. My memory of him was like that old Greek sea-god Proteus who turned into someone else every time anyone nearly pinned him down. Without a sight of Jack, I felt as if Simon had been a character in a soap opera, someone unreal but somehow authenticated because he was the focus of real mass emotion. And as I lost touch with the man I still loved, I began to doubt the reality of my own identity as well as his.

I'd always let his public persona overwhelm my own. I knew I'd allowed the supposed dictates of his career to dominate my life as well as his. It was hard to accept that the relationship I'd seen as a basis for my whole future was built on an illusion of my own making.

I sometimes wondered if losing touch with Simon this way had anything to do with my obsession with ruining Karen's apparent happiness. He was real to her. By accusing Simon of rape, she'd done something concrete, something solid and real and full of hatred. That proved he was real to her, the real object of her real hatred. I'd come to believe that I could only recapture my sense of Simon as a real person by destroying Karen's possession of any part of him. And this wasn't going to happen while Karen was alive. Karen had to die.

At the time, none of this seemed weird to me. I thought it was absolutely logical. I hated it that all I'd achieved so far was to create Karen as the real person. She'd become an emotional squatter in my head to the point that Simon wasn't really the issue any more. I had to eradicate Karen before I could deal with Simon's loss and take back control of my own life.

My thoughts were so concentrated on Karen as I walked slowly up the village street that at first I didn't notice her waiting outside the post office for the bus to town. She was chatting to a group of older women with shopping baskets. They were laughing and their laughter made me remember how long it was since I'd laughed like that.

I turned away and pretended to study the times of mail collections in the post-office window, but I could see the object of my hatred reflected in the glass.

If only, I thought, if I could break this glass and it would destroy not just Karen's image but the reality of her existence so she, too, would become a mere illusion. Some hope! Break the glass, shatter the reflection, and she'd be there, large as life, behind my back, laughing with those village women.

The bus arrived. I watched her climb aboard with the others. I heard her ask for a ticket to town. I watched the bus disappear at the far end of the village street. Then I ran back to The Black Bull to pick up my car.

There was no sign of anyone out and about to see where I was going. The previous day's rain had turned the track to the Midgley farm into a racing stream, spilling debris and small boulders on to the road. Before long I had to leave the car and walk.

As I climbed slowly up the hill, I asked myself what I thought I was going to get out of this pointless route march. I kept telling myself that I didn't have to go on. My feet were soaked; the sodden legs of my jeans slapped my ankles; my eyes watered and stung as I clambered into the wind up the bleak fellside. But I kept going.

I had to *know*.

Know what? I asked myself.

I couldn't say.

I'd know when I found what it was. Then I'd know what I was going to do to her. Whatever it was I was hoping to find, I wanted it to seal her fate, a justification for her death.

The farmhouse looked like a ruin when I finally reached it. The place seemed empty. The front door had been boarded and nailed. At one end of the building, a corner of the wall had collapsed. It must have been like that for years; brambles were growing out of the crumbled stones.

I walked round the side of the house and looked in through a ground-floor window. The room inside was vast, sparsely furnished with a heavy dark table and four assorted dining chairs which created a small island in the centre of the expanse of bare floorboards.

There was no sign of life.

The rear of the house was protected from the wind by the rocky fell that rose steeply behind it. Here there were some signs of attempts at ordinary life, at least there were culinary herbs growing higgledy-piggledy in a small plot outside the back door, and a few bedraggled flowers still bloomed in pots around a paved patio.

I knocked on the door. It was like touching wood for luck. I was sure there was no one there, but best behave as if there were. Double checking – that was the sub-editor in me coming out; subs were born, not made. But after all, Karen's peasant swain, Andy Little, might have stayed over, though there wasn't any sign of his pickup.

No one answered my knock, of course. I turned a corroded brass knob and the door opened.

'Hello,' I shouted, 'is anyone there?'

No answer.

I walked into a large, white-painted kitchen with a flagged floor scattered with bright-coloured rag rugs. On this dank, wintry day, there wasn't much light in the room. I turned on the electric switch, but nothing happened. I saw several oil lamps standing inside the back door. The place must be prone to power cuts, it was so exposed. Or perhaps Karen, distracted by the triumph of her campaign against Simon, had forgotten to pay the bill. It did occur to me that perhaps Karen and Jean Midgley couldn't afford to pay it, but then why hadn't Karen cashed in on her Simon West story at once? She couldn't be in that much of a hurry for money.

Peering into the gloom, I made out an ancient Esse cooker, and an old-fashioned Belfast sink. Heavy blackened copper saucepans hung from the walls near the stove. A child's paintings, crude and colourful, adorned the wall facing the window. A half-eaten sandwich lay on the draining board with an upturned mug and an almost empty bottle of whisky.

There was an old armchair by the stove, covered in a flow-ered chintz. It at least looked cheerful and oddly enough in spite of the obvious poverty, the place was warm and welcoming. It wasn't what I'd expected, though I'm not sure what that was. Something like a witch's hovel, I suppose.

On the enormous kitchen table someone had been working on a model aeroplane. There was a gluepot and a cluster of scattered model plane parts on the scrubbed wood surface. The model looked complicated, not yet much like the large coloured photograph on the box which lay beside it as a guide.

Jack wasn't much like his father, then. Simon could never do anything like that. Before I'd seen the child's toy, I'd felt I had some kind of right to be there, a kind of family connection, but the unfinished model aeroplane made me feel like a spy.

In a dark corner of the room, a grandfather clock ticked then suddenly chimed the hour. It startled me, and I nearly turned and ran out of the house. I could feel my heart thumping as I held my breath, but nothing stirred. Then once again the only sound was the heavy ticking of the clock.

I explored further into the house. Apart from the kitchen, the downstairs rooms were scarcely furnished. Some were entirely empty. Karen and Jack plainly spent most of their time in the kitchen. I'd do the same if I lived there, it would cost a fortune to heat every room in this place.

Upstairs, above the kitchen, I found Karen's bedroom.

A denim skirt and several sweaters had been thrown on the double bed, where the bedding had been hastily pulled up over the pillows. An alarm clock on the bedside table was set for 6.30.

The room had a spectacular view across the valley to the hills beyond. I could see the roofs of Brockbeck in the distance, but there was no sign of any other building in sight. I realized why I'd thought the house was empty; there were no curtains at the windows. The casements still had their original wooden shutters, which looked as though they hadn't been closed for years. But this house could be beautiful. Done up, it was the sort of place I'd dreamed that Simon and I might have owned one day, a real family home.

I touched the personal things on Karen's dressing-table. And I stood for some time looking at myself in the mirror. I even used Karen's lipstick on my mouth and smeared Karen's pale-grey eye shadow on my lids. The colours didn't suit me. My colouring is mousy, but much darker than Karen.

I didn't look anything like her, so what had Simon seen in me after her? In fact, what had Simon seen in me not only after Karen, but after Marta Blane as well? They were both beautiful, and I wasn't even pretty. Why should someone as image conscious and, yes, as vain as Simon have wanted to be seen with someone like me. Well, he hadn't actually wanted to be seen with me. I was his secret and I was safe, that was why, he hadn't felt threatened by me. That was what love had meant to him, security. And what was wrong with that, if it was what he'd wanted?

I pushed that thought roughly out of my head and returned to exploring the bedroom of my hated enemy. I was breathing very fast and my hands trembled. It was dangerously exciting being here, in my enemy's bedroom knowing that if she came back at this moment and found me I would kill her, I couldn't stop myself. But would I get away with it? Did anyone know I'd ever been here? Better not take an opportunity, I'd bide my time and plan her death.

There were several framed photographs on the dressing-table. The largest showed an old man and a younger woman who must've been Jean Midgley, a laughing, fresh-faced girl-without the garish make up and the brassy hair of the raddled woman I knew from The Black Bull. Except for the old-fashioned clothes and hairstyle, it could have been a picture of Karen now.

Two or three photos of Jack at various ages made me smile.

He looked a happy kid. For a moment I wondered how right of me it was to destroy his mother, he'd only have his drunken grandmother then. I wouldn't let that happen, I'd take care of that when the time came.

There was one studio portrait of Karen. She was wearing an evening dress and she had a secret little smile on her face as though she was going to meet her lover. The back of my neck went suddenly cold as I looked at the picture.

I picked up another photo and I saw Simon. He was at the front of a group of young men in sporting gear. He and another man were holding a large silver cup above their heads. They were laughing. Behind them, among an excited crowd, Karen was waving her arms above her head in jubilation.

She was heavily pregnant.

I turned and ran down the stairs and out of the back door, not looking back. I sped across the scree on the side of the fell, trying to escape from that image of Simon and Karen happy together. I didn't realize until I was 200 yards at least from the house that I had taken the photograph with me. I was clutching it in my left hand and when I tried to drop it, I couldn't. I forced myself to look at it again: Simon laughed up at me, and behind him Karen was jubilant – and pregnant!

I knew I must return it. Karen would miss it. She'd know someone had been in her house, spying on her. She knew she'd caused Simon's death, so what would she think when the picture of the two of them together suddenly disappeared? And nothing else taken. She'd know someone knew about her and what she'd done and was after her. She'd begin to be afraid. I didn't want that, not yet. I wasn't ready yet.

I looked at my watch. There was still some time before Karen's bus could be due back in Brockbeck. I scrambled painfully up the hill I'd descended at such speed. Stumbling, sweat dripping off my brows into my eyes, my legs weak with effort, I reached the farmhouse. Upstairs, I put the photograph back where I'd found it.

The Karen of the studio portrait gave me a smug little smile. 'Be afraid,' I hissed at her, 'I'm going to wipe that smile off your evil face.'

21

Getting Even

Notional threats were one thing, but the kind of action which would really make Karen suffer was another.

Such thoughts tormented me in sleepless hours before dawn. Simply, I'd convinced myself that the only way to achieve the catharsis I needed before I could return to real life was to destroy Karen. I wasn't specific about how to do this; I didn't actually see myself strangling the life out of her. I wanted her to be alive and suffering. I wanted to make her wish she was dead.

She wasn't the only one who'd helped destroy Simon, but it was a waste of effort trying to take revenge on the police or the media, or even the mindless public. Karen Midgley, though, could be made to suffer.

The question was how.

That was what I lay in bed in the dark and thought about. And in my dreams, too, I acted out means of doing away with Karen in ways which involved some slow process of suffering before she died. My sleeping hours became more real than the slow-moving reality of daytime.

'Where does Andy Little live?' I asked Doreen one morning.

'Does he come into your research?'

Doreen had an irritating habit of answering one question with another. It probably made her a good gossip, but it wasn't much use to anyone wanting simple information.

'Should he?' I was beginning to learn the trick.

'How's your work here going?' Doreen said, her eyes narrowing. 'I'm afraid things aren't going well for your research. I wonder if you haven't been misled about your man's connections with this area.'

She was defensive. If I hadn't found what I was looking for in Brockbeck, it wasn't going to be Brockbeck's fault. Why couldn't the bloody woman give a simple answer to a simple question? In my dreams I might be committing the perfect murder every night, but in real life I was drawing attention to a connection with Karen with my questions, and this link would make me into a suspect if Karen were killed.

I asked Doreen again, 'Where does Andy Little live? Karen said she might be there later. But she forgot to give me the address.'

'She's agreed to talk to you, then? You could have talked to her here last night, she and Andy came in for a drink.'

'Yes,' I said, 'I saw them. I think they'd got something private to talk about.'

'That's true.'

It was a concession. She gave me directions. Andy Little lived in a cottage on a large farm on the road out of Brockbeck. His parents lived in the farmhouse and Andy and his father ran the farm together. According to Doreen, when Andy got married he and his new wife would take over the farmhouse and the old people would retire to the cottage.

I drove slowly down the main road past the entrance to the Little farm. Once again that surname was confusing, for it was a substantial place; an imposing square granite house and extensive outbuildings. A large herd of Friesian cows was waiting in a covered yard to be let out to pasture. I didn't see a cottage. I began to look for a place to turn the car to go back for a second look.

I was backing into a track in a small wood when I saw in the driving mirror that this was the entrance to a stone cottage set well back among the trees. I recognized the pickup truck parked outside. Andy Little and John had loaded the drunken Jean into it the night I'd seen him take her home.

The curtains were closed at an upstairs window. As I watched, they were pulled back and Karen Midgley, naked, threw open the casement. She stood there for a moment, breathing in the fresh air, then disappeared back into the room.

She really was beautiful, much more beautiful than me. Than I, the sub-editor in me corrected – I, much, much more beautiful than I. It seemed to me that Simon couldn't have stopped himself loving someone as beautiful as that.

If I'd had any doubts about what I was going to do, that glimpse of Karen Midgley's beauty naked as Simon must have seen her decided me. I couldn't go back now.

I drove to Alderdale, a market town about fifteen miles from Brockbeck. This was apparently where the Brockbeck children went to school. I daydreamed about what I'd do if I ran into Jack. Nothing, I told myself sternly, I wasn't ready for thoughts like that yet, these were the early stages. I concentrated on Alderdale like a gangster casing the joint, except the place was no Chicago. There was a library there, a department store and three supermarkets, that was all. And there was a daily newspaper.

I walked into the newspaper office. First I asked for the area telephone directory and wrote down the number I wanted.

'I want to put a notice in tonight's paper,' I told the girl behind the counter.

'How many words?' the girl asked. She handed me a form without looking at me.

'I'll know when I've written it,' I said. She gave me a black look then, or as close to a black look as a sugary-sweet big blue-eyed blonde wearing baby pink can manage.

I wrote down what I wanted to say.

'Here,' I said to Miss Sugar-Sweet, 'you add it up.'

The girl began to read, counting the words on her fingers.

'Is this what you want to say?' she asked at last. 'Are you sure?'

'Yes,' I said. 'It's not a bad living if you don't weaken.' Why did I say that? I asked myself, I didn't have to justify anything to this Barbie doll.

She gave me a hard look. 'People could misunderstand what "Intimate personal service" means.'

I said, 'No, I don't think so, that says exactly what I mean.'

She shrugged her angora shoulders. 'That'll be ten pounds,' she said.

As she waited for me to pay, she slipped a small diamond engagement ring up and down on her finger. I know a gesture of moral superiority when I see it.

'I'd break the engagement off, if I were you,' I said, 'I'm sure you can do better for yourself. I wouldn't be seen dead with such a small stone, I wouldn't accept it as a tip.'

I left before the girl could recover from her shock.

Serve her right, prim little bitch. But why did I do that? The vapid little cow hadn't done me any harm. What was the matter with me? Was I going crazy? It was Karen I was trying to destabilize, not that pathetic little tart with her spotty boyfriend. I'd been stupid, too, I'd made sure the girl would remember me. If I could make a mistake like that organizing a warning shot, how was I going to get away with murder?

As I drove back to Brockbeck the question of my own sanity nagged like toothache. I'd started something grotesque. If I'd heard of someone else doing what I'd done, I wouldn't hesitate. I'd say that person was mad.

'But I'm not mad,' I said aloud, 'I'm only getting even.'

22

A Local Item

John and Doreen were sitting having coffee in the bar when I came down the next morning. The local paper was spread between them. They were talking in fierce whispers and when I appeared, they looked guilty and pushed the paper away from them.

'Good morning,' I said. 'Something interesting in that paper for once?'

They both started to speak.

'No, nothing really,' said John. 'Just local interest.'

'It's a scandal. It can't be true,' said Doreen.

'What's happened?' I said. I could scarcely keep a straight face.

I sat down between them at the table and pulled the paper towards me.

'I've work to do, if no one else does,' John said.

He got up and went out into the kitchen, where he began to make a lot of noise.

'It's an advertisement. It must be some sort of hoax. I don't believe it,' Doreen said.

'Hey, show me,' I said. 'What kind of advert?'

Doreen started to fold the paper with her bony fingers so that I couldn't read it without being rude.

'No, it must be a hoax,' she said. But the gossip's instinct was too strong. She hesitated, then muttered, 'It says Karen's reopening her business providing gentlemen with discreet personal services of an intimate nature.' Doreen flushed. 'At a new address.'

'Karen's a common name,' I said. 'Lots of that sort of girls are called Karen.'

'It's not just that,' Doreen said. Her face was red. 'It's the address and telephone number where . . . well, it says she's running this disgusting business from Little's farm.'

Doreen paused, then delivered her *coup de grâce*.

'Old Mr Little is a lay preacher. He's a Methodist,' she said.

'Really?' I said. 'He doesn't sound like most Methodists I've ever known, not if he doesn't mind Karen offering her services from his own home.' Careful, I told myself, don't overplay your hand.

'Doesn't mind?' Doreen cried. 'They'll never get over it. But of course it's not true. Word of Andy's engagement to Karen must've got around. Someone who wants Andy Little for herself must be behind this. That's most unmarried girls in the village.'

'Maybe some of them are disappointed, but who'd actually do such a thing?' I asked.

'What a shame, too, this coming just as Andy and Karen seemed to be getting things sorted at last,' Doreen said. 'That girl's had a hard time, and this could cause no end of trouble, everyone taking sides and suspecting each other.'

'But they'll know it's a hoax, won't they? Brockbeck's a small community. Surely people couldn't be vicious enough to believe it of a girl like Karen. How could they believe it?'

I sounded so innocent I told myself I'd missed my vocation; I should've been an actress.

'You're a city girl,' Doreen said. 'You don't have any idea what goes on in a village like this.'

'No smoke without fire, you mean?' Suddenly I thought of that bitch Fortuny and I wasn't laughing any more, the old helpless anger was back. 'That's what they'll think, isn't it?' I said to Doreen. 'That's human nature for you. But don't worry, most people probably won't see it. I don't suppose many locals read those sex ads, do you?'

'You'd be surprised,' she said.

By the time the bar opened in the evening, I knew that Doreen wasn't mistaken. Practically everyone who came in carried a copy of the newspaper and the sole topic of conversation was muttered discussion of the advertisement. Or rather, as I realized when my ear was finally tuned to what was being said, the discussion was about what would happen next. No one seemed to doubt that Karen was a whore. After all, she'd fallen pregnant with Jack and hadn't been married to the father, whoever he was. In Brockbeck, that tended to mean that Karen didn't know who the father was. Ergo she was a whore.

I, too, was carried away by a weird logic of my own. I found myself thinking about poor Jack. What kind of life was he going to have with a mother like Karen and a drunken tart for a grandmother? Suddenly, and quite unexpectedly, I felt protective towards the boy.

But he'd be better off without Karen, better off with someone more able to take care of him. I'd make sure he was all right when this was over. Simon would want that.

Filled with sentimental thoughts, I sat in the corner of the bar watching as Karen Midgley's reputation was ripped to shreds. I hadn't expected the gleeful venom with which these people turned against one of their own.

Then I noticed Jean Midgley slumped on a barstool.

She was dressed to pull, in a black see-through blouse over the sort of bra only available from a mail order catalogue. She'd kicked off gold stiletto-heeled sandals, and a tight red leather miniskirt had no chance of hiding a large hole in the top of her black stocking.

I wanted to laugh at the drunken witch making a spectacle of herself, but somehow I couldn't. And then I became aware that some of the locals were goading the woman, asking her with leering innuendo about Karen's professional qualifications, and where she'd learned her trade.

'Do you think she'd give a special rate for groups?' asked a laughing man.

His ruddy face glistened with sweat. He was wearing a rugby-club shirt. I'd seen him before with Andy Little. He and his friends guffawed. Jean Midgley looked confused.

'Where's your Karen's Andy tonight, Jean?' a young woman in the group asked. 'Oh, I forgot, he'll be enjoying a few home comforts before the rush hour starts.'

'Teach her the tricks of the trade yourself, did you, Jean?' someone called out from the back of the crowd.

An old man leered at her.

'Want to show 'em how, Jean, for old times' sake?' he asked.

Jean Midgley was too drunk to turn on them. She sat with her arms splayed on the bar top as though embracing the line of drinks her tormenters had been buying for her to loosen her tongue. They wanted to see what she would do when they made her lose her temper.

Jean turned her head and I saw her face. Tears flowed down her rouged cheeks. Her mascara had run so that her thick make-up looked like cracked parchment.

This was obscene. It wasn't fair. I must stop it. I stood up to go to her. But before I could move, there was a sudden

149

hush and the crowd fell back.

Karen Midgley and Andy Little came into the bar and pushed their way to Jean's side.

Karen, shining, fresh as mountain air in the gloomy, stale-smelling pub, put her arm round her mother's shoulders.

'It's OK, Mum, we're here now. Andy and I will look after you.'

She turned and glared at the group of drinkers around her mother. Someone laughed, then there was silence.

Jean Midgley smiled at her daughter. With Karen's help she got to her feet and turned to go. Her lopsided lipstick mouth worked as she spoke.

'You lot should be ashamed,' she said, her words slurred but the meaning plain. 'I was a whore and I'm not ashamed of it. But my Karen's a good girl and she's shown the lot of you, you rotten dirty bastards. There's not one of you fit to touch her.'

Andy Little put his arm around Karen's shoulders and held her against him. 'We're engaged,' he said, 'we're going to be married and if there's someone in this bar who doesn't like it, I'm warning them now, they're wasting their time trying to break us up.'

There was a moment's silence, then everyone was shouting. The vicious innuendo might never have existed, Karen was restored to adulation. Behind the bar, John bellowed that the drinks were on him.

Jean clung to Karen.

'You can't leave me,' I heard her whisper to Karen, 'you can't go away and leave me alone in that house.'

'Of course not, Mum, there's no question of it.'

'But what's going to happen to me, Karen?'

'Not now, Mum.'

I saw the happiness drain out of Karen's face. She kept smiling, but as I watched her, I was in no doubt that Jean

Midgley was a problem that Karen and Andy had not even begun to resolve.

She was Karen's weak spot; I saw a way I could get at my enemy, through that awful mother.

23

Saying it with Flowers

So next day I was on my way to the market town of Alderdale once more. I was excited, full of anticipation. I missed Simon, but suddenly it wasn't with the old gnawing ache. I simply wished he was there to share the fun.

I went first to the Alderdale branch of my bank. I took £250 out of the cash machine because what I was going to do required money and I had to pay cash. A cheque or credit card could easily be traced back to me. Two hundred and fifty pounds was a lot of money, but I didn't think twice about it. I was carried away by the excitement of the chase.

I found the florist I wanted, attached to the one luxury hotel in the centre of town. Hotel guests, strangers, came and went; I wasn't likely to be remembered. I wasn't going to repeat my past mistakes and give people reason to remember me. I blamed myself for mentioning Karen when I first came to the village, and now I wasn't going to be so careless again.

'My name's Karen Midgley,' I said to the saleswoman. I spelt out the surname. I gave Andy Little's address.

I asked for cards and wrote out several messages. 'I'm doing this for all the close family,' I said, handing them to the saleswoman. 'At a time like this . . .'

'Mum's to be spelled out in lilies, is that right?'

'As long as it's nice and dignified.'

I was enjoying myself. I picked out the flowers with real care. I found my eyes were wet with tears of real sorrow.

It didn't seem to me that what I was doing was in the least unbalanced. I felt no guilt. Karen deserved it. Let her believe she'd lost someone close. And there was the extra twist that I was certain that the first shock would be followed by a feeling of relief, and the guilt of that would make her feel even worse.

And I was having a good time, surely I couldn't enjoy doing something really wrong?

Back in Brockbeck, I left my car at The Black Bull and began to wander around the village. Actually, I was searching for Karen. I wanted to be close to her, savouring the pain I'd planned for her.

She was in the post office chatting to a few village women while she paid a utility bill. They were still talking about the newspaper advert.

'Who'd do a thing like that?' the postmistress said.

'I don't know,' Karen said. She sounded weary. 'Someone sick in the head.' Clearly she wanted to get away.

'There are some very sick minds about,' another woman said.

'Well, whoever it is, it didn't work,' Karen said. She smiled at the postmistress. 'Andy's parents were so shocked by the malice, they want us to get married at once.'

'Isn't that nice,' the postmistress said. 'Real Christian folk.'

Karen turned and saw the pickup truck coming up the street. 'There's Andy, I must go,' she said. She became confiding. 'I'm cooking for his parents tonight. He's dropping me back to the cottage now so I can get on with it. My first dinner for the in-laws, and I'm terrified. Mrs Little's a marvellous cook. Wish me luck.'

She went out and ran to meet Andy in the pickup.

The village women and the postmistress gathered closer.

'She's been staying up there in the woods with him since the beginning of the week,' one said.

'If you ask me it's not any hoaxer's malice as has shocked the old Littles,' said the postmistress, 'it's that hussy and her goings on. They're afraid of another little bastard on the way.'

'Don't you mean a Little bastard?' one of the women said, and they all laughed.

'If they're really letting young Andy marry that tart without a fight, it must be because she's pregnant.'

'Wouldn't put it past her.'

'You don't mean . . . using the baby to force. . . ? Oh, surely she wouldn't do anything like that?'

'We know what sort of girl Karen Midgley is. There's the lad to prove it.'

'And it's there in the genes. With Jean Midgley for a mother what could you expect?'

I picked up a packet of mints and took them to the counter to pay.

'Is that the girl who advertised in the paper?' I asked. 'The one everyone's talking about?'

All the women stared at me. They were affronted. I'd overstepped the mark.

'I don't know anything about that, I'm sure,' said the postmistress. She handed me change and turned away.

Outside the shop, I said aloud, 'To hell with the old cats anyway.'

'Sorry?' said a young woman with a pushchair.

I laughed. 'Talking to myself in the street,' I said. 'You know what they say about that?'

The girl gave me a sideways look and hurried on.

154

She didn't see I was joking. She probably thought I was actually crazy. But then no one was normal round there, as far as I could see.

I felt suddenly nostalgic for the busy camaraderie of the *Gazette* office and the crowded bars and streets of Castleborough. The people in this grim grey place were like the granite they sprang from, cold and impenetrable. Karen alone of them all wasn't like that. She didn't fit in there.

That must've been why the scheming bitch accused Simon, as a way of using him to get herself out of Brockbeck. That was what she'd wanted the money for. She'd probably thought he'd pay her off.

I had no qualms about what I was doing; it was only fair. In fact what I was doing now was nowhere near what I intended to do in taking revenge.

But it was time to go. I drove out of the village towards Andy Little's cottage. On my way I passed the pickup speeding back towards Brockbeck. So far so good. It was better that Karen should be alone.

Once past the farm and the wood surrounding the cottage, I parked the car out of sight in a gateway down a track off the main road. Then I made my way back through a hazel copse until I could watch the front of the cottage with little chance of being seen.

I was only just in time. Before I'd settled in my hiding place, the florist's van arrived at Andy Little's front door.

The driver jumped down and opened the back doors of the van. Then he went and banged at the cottage door.

Karen came out. She'd been washing her hair, there was a red towel wrapped round her head.

She looked good, even like that.

I couldn't hear what the driver said. I saw Karen's look of shock. The driver was gesticulating, pulling flowers out and pushing them into Karen's arms. I heard Karen protesting.

'No, no, it can't be,' she said. The tribute to Mum, all white lilies and lugubrious laurel, was laid against the cottage wall. They'd done a good job at the shop, that enormous pile of flowers looked like they were for a London East End gangster's send-off.

Karen was trying to refuse to take the flowers. But the driver showed her a form, and took up cards from the flower arrangements. Karen looked at them. She was very pale.

She wasn't so confident now, not after she'd seen there was no mistake, the flowers were ordered in her name. And paid for. That one with yellow roses was the wreath from Jack; the chrysanthemums were from the Little parents. I was pleased with my choice of flowers.

The florist's van drove off. Karen stood amid a heap of funeral flowers. She was worried.

I gloated at the sight of her stricken face.

She didn't know what to do. She couldn't phone to see if her mother was at home, the farm wasn't on the telephone. She daren't phone the old Littles to see if they'd heard anything in case Jean was dead and they'd be shocked she was such a negligent daughter she didn't know. I felt real pleasure, watching her. Good, let her suffer. It was nothing compared to what she'd made Simon and me go through.

I watched her run into the house. I was excited, full of expectation.

Karen reappeared almost at once wearing a coat and boots, her wet hair loose on her shoulders. She ran to the road and hurried away in the direction of Brockbeck.

I walked back to my car, deliberately slowly, and set off towards the village. I saw Karen half-running, half-walking, on the road ahead. I drove past her, then stopped and backed, leaning across to open the nearside door.

'Do you want a lift? I'm going to Brockbeck.'

Seeing Karen hesitate, I said, 'We were both in the post

office earlier. I'm staying at The Black Bull.'

Then she recognized me. 'Thanks,' she said, getting into the car.

She was breathless. Her face was pinched and white in spite of running up the road.

When she was seated in the car, I asked, 'Is something wrong?'

Karen shook her head. 'I forgot something I had to do. I've got to go home.'

I thought I could actually smell her fear, but it was probably shampoo and the perfume she was wearing, no doubt put on specially for Andy.

'Where's home?' I asked. We were entering the village now.

'Oh, I can walk from the pub, if you'll drop me there.'

'Nonsense,' I said. I heard myself sounding like a school prefect. 'I've a car and nothing much to do and you're in a hurry, anyone can see that. Of course I'll take you home.'

Karen looked relieved. 'Thanks,' she said, 'if you don't mind. It's that way.'

She pointed the way up the rough road I knew so well.

She wasn't going to tell me what had happened, she was feeling too guilty to admit it. Good.

Karen seemed to pull herself together and remember her manners.

'Are you on holiday?' she asked. 'It's not the best time of year for sightseeing.'

'No, I'm researching a book,' I said.

'A book? What about?'

'Simon West.'

The car bucked over a boulder, making us both gasp.

'Sorry,' I said, 'the springs in this car aren't what they were.'

Karen's face was a blank.

'Simon West? The one who was on television?'

She sounded as though she was being very careful what she said. 'Why come here to do that? Did he have connections here?'

I took care, too, that my face gave nothing away.

I paused, then said, 'I was told he had. But no one here seems to know anything about him. Actually, I thought you might be able to help. I heard you were once in television yourself.'

'I never heard anyone say anything,' Karen said. She was definitely wary now, if not scared. 'Could you drop me here,' she said. 'I'll be faster walking. The going gets pretty difficult from now on, but it's no distance on foot. You can turn and go back down.'

'Don't you want me to wait and take you back?'

'No,' Karen said too loudly. Then she said more calmly, 'No, thanks all the same. I'll be fine now.'

Damn, just as I was about to start pinning her down.

'I can easily wait.'

'Please, don't think of it. You've already gone out of your way.'

Karen made no effort to disguise her eagerness to be rid of me. I was pleased that I'd certainly rattled my quarry. She was behaving as though she thought I'd got an ulterior motive, like I wanted to kidnap Jack or something. Well, let her worry.

'I'll be in touch, then, about Simon West,' I said. 'You must've come across him at some stage if you were in television. At least you'll know people who knew him.'

'No, I can't help you,' Karen said. 'Thanks for the lift.'

If she thought she could get rid of me that easily, she'd got another think coming.

I made a great production out of turning the car so I could watch her go into the farmhouse. I heard her shout for her

158

mother as she opened the front door. There was panic in her voice.

I couldn't help smiling as I drove slowly back to the village. There's some theory that you can make yourself feel happy if you go through the motions of smiling, but I think that's rubbish. You've got to feel happy before you can really smile. I did.

It was only much later, alone in my room at The Black Bull, that I recalled Karen's stricken face as she stood amid the funeral flowers and I felt a pang of guilt. But what I'd done was nothing compared to what she did to Simon. Even so, I was glad Jack wasn't there to see her look like that. It would have frightened him.

Karen had looked as if she thought she was going mad, as if she wasn't sure what she was doing any more. I was getting to her. I could drive her insane. 'Or go crazy in the attempt myself,' I said aloud.

24

Trouble in the Family

In the bar of the pub, Jean Midgley and two ancient men were trying to sing. But once they'd howled the refrain of the song none of them knew any more of the words, so they sang it again and again. Other drinkers moved away, trying to escape the noise.

'Keep the din down,' John shouted at them. 'I don't have a licence for music.'

'You don't need one. That's not bloody music,' Doreen told him.

'Where's Karen?' John asked Jean. He was plainly hoping she might come in and take her mother home.

'Shagging the shit out of that fellow of hers, I expect.' Jean winked and licked her oddly painted lips. 'That's what I'd be doing if I got the chance,' she said.

'Fat chance of that,' Doreen muttered under her breath.

'When do they tie the knot?' someone asked.

'Over my dead body,' Jean said, 'and I'm not dead yet.' Tears trickled down her rouged cheeks. 'If I'd wanted that Andy Little,' she snarled, 'I could've had him, just like that.' She tried to snap her fingers, but nothing happened.

There was a sudden disturbance at the far end of the bar. The street door banged open. Andy and Karen were struggling in the doorway. She was carrying a huge bouquet of white flowers. He was trying to hold her back.

'Let me go,' she shouted at him. 'This is between me and her.'

'Karen, don't do this,' Andy said, 'there's no point.'

She shook her head.

'Please, Andy, just wait outside in the pickup.'

He hesitated, then turned and left.

Karen marched up to her mother. She threw the flowers on to the bar.

'Here,' she said, 'you might as well have these. After all, you paid for them.'

No one in the bar spoke. They were all watching Jean, who stared at the flowers, as though wondering what they were.

Then she started to pick the petals off one of the blooms. She stared at Karen, saying nothing.

Karen watched her. 'How could you do it, Mum?' she said. She started to cry.

Behind the bar, Doreen moved forward and picked up the flowers. 'They're beautiful,' she said.

'They're funeral flowers,' Jean Midgley said, sounding sober again.

'Yes,' Karen hissed at her, 'flowers for your funeral, you sick cow.'

'I'm not dead yet,' Jean said. 'I was just saying that. I said "I'm not dead yet", you heard me, John.'

'That's right, Jean,' John said. He was worried about a fight starting.

'So why did you send a load of funeral flowers to Andy's place for your bloody burial?' Karen said. She couldn't stop her voice wobbling. 'Did you want to frighten me because I

161

was staying over with him?'

'I didn't,' Jean said. 'I didn't send nothing.'

'Mum, I rang the florists and they said *I'd* come in and chosen them. They couldn't remember me, but they had the record of sale in my name. You told them you were me. You must've done. Who else would do a thing like that?'

I tried to keep my face blank, but it was hard not to laugh.

John came out from behind the bar and pushed his way between Jean and Karen at the counter.

'I don't want trouble here. You sort out your family feuds somewhere else.'

'Not me,' Jean said. 'It wasn't me.'

Doreen said, 'Karen, I know you're upset, but, honestly, look at these flowers. Where would Jean get the money to pay for this kind of thing?'

'She finds plenty of money for drink, doesn't she?' Karen shouted at her. 'It's only when it comes to me and Jack there's never a penny to spare.'

Doreen was startled at Karen's vehemence.

She said, 'Stop it, Karen, this is getting out of hand. You'll be sorry you said anything tomorrow.'

Karen took a deep breath.

Then she said, 'Mum, you've got to try to understand. I'm going to marry Andy whatever you do to try and stop me.'

'No,' Jean said, 'no, no, no.'

25

I Burn a Photograph

I lay awake in bed early next morning going over in my head what had happened in the bar the previous night.

It had never been part of my plan for Karen to accuse her mother of being her persecutor. It was pure luck that Karen thought her tormentor was Jean.

At least she was getting some idea of Simon's helplessness in the face of malice from someone he'd loved. Of course she didn't connect what was happening to her with what she'd done to Simon, I still had that to do, but she was certainly suffering.

Why, then, did I still feel so empty?

I'd hoped that in hurting Karen Midgley I'd reclaim Simon for myself. But he was more distant now than ever. There remained that vast emptiness at the centre of my life. I couldn't see any future for myself. All my existence was now contained in my obsession with destroying Karen's happiness.

I asked myself why, if I couldn't get closer to Simon through Karen, did I feel I must go on? I just had to, that's why. I didn't know how to stop.

What would Simon think of me? Would he be glad that Karen was being punished?

I knew the answer to that.

Simon would have hated what I was doing. He wouldn't want revenge. He'd never wanted to punish Karen.

So how could I feel so driven to get retribution for him if that was true?

I didn't even try to answer that question.

I was suddenly overwhelmed by longing for Simon. I put out my hand under the bedclothes to touch him, as though he were only hidden in the dark. 'My darling,' I whispered, 'I miss you so much.' The sheet was cold.

Early as it was, there was no point in lying there feeling lonely. I dressed and went downstairs. John was clearing up in the bar. He was very pink in the face and I could hear him breathing heavily. I wondered if Doreen worried that he was getting too fat for his own good. Stringy little women like Doreen lived for ever, but John looked and sounded like a classic cardiac arrest waiting to happen.

'That was quite a scene last night,' I said, to make conversation.

'Poor woman,' John said. 'It's a cruel life for a woman like Jean Midgley to lose her looks.'

I was irritated by this new sensitivity of his. Was there nothing people wouldn't forgive the Midgleys?

'Was she OK?'

John shrugged. 'She and old Bart were the last to leave,' he said. 'He wouldn't let her come to any harm. Probably they both went back to his cottage for a few more drinks and passed out in their chairs. It wouldn't be the first time, and them not the only ones, neither.'

I quailed at this vision of the rural idyll.

John put a tray of dirty glasses on the counter. 'I think that's the lot,' he said. 'What've you got in mind for today?'

'Oh,' I said, 'this and that. I might go for a walk if the weather looks good. I've no set plan.'

But I had. I knew exactly what I was going to do.

I set out to walk up the track towards the Midgley farm.

A blustery wind in the night had dried the ground. After a while I began to enjoy the walk. A group of sheep grazing on the fell turned and fled up the hill when they saw me, leaping from boulder to boulder like goats. Above my head, against a grey sky, a hawk soared, riding the wind.

The farm, when I reached it, was deserted. A few chickens scratching on a dung heap were the only sign of life.

I went round to the back door as though the house were the home of a familiar friend.

The door wasn't locked. I opened it and walked in.

The place felt as though it had been abandoned for days.

The kitchen looked exactly as it had when I'd been there days ago.

I went straight upstairs to Karen's bedroom. I felt I had a right to be there.

I pushed aside the formal studio portrait of Karen to pick up the photograph of Simon laughing with his pregnant girl-friend smiling in the crowd. He looked happy among his friends. His eyes, as he held the trophy aloft, seemed to be on Karen. But then, most of the other men in the picture seemed to be looking at her too. Perhaps she'd just said something, asked a question, made a joke. I stared at her face in the photograph. She looked happy. But why wouldn't she?

As I studied the picture, it was as though the judgemental Karen of the studio portrait watched me. This supercilious Karen knew her own strength. Cool and superior, she smiled her secret lover's smile and mocked me.

I'd never known before what it was like to be carried away by any emotion except love. I had felt that kind of over-whelming love for Simon, and even in the last few dreadful weeks when I often dreaded seeing him, that irresistible passion remained with me both as solace and a kind of promise. But what I felt now was relentless and terrifying; my hatred became a kind of inverted glorification.

I smashed the picture frame. Shards of glass glittered on the floor. Suddenly I was screaming. I was screaming and at the same time I was watching myself screaming in Karen's mirror as though it had nothing to do with me. My screaming self was trying to express the helpless, furious frustration that consumed me; but the spectator self knew the pointlessness of such expression. There was no human sound, no civilized action, which would have given vent to what was inside me.

Then I was in the kitchen. I had the portrait of Karen in my hand.

It was as though this was my own home; I knew where to find what I wanted. The oil lamp by the back door, matches from the drawer under the sink, the model aeroplane's box, kindling in a pile beside the Esse, all seemed familiar.

I took off the blackened glass funnel on the lamp and lit the wick. The flame flared, blue, pale green and yellow; cleansing fire, pure, cauterizing. I put the edge of Karen's face into the flame, and held the photograph as the fire twisted and turned it so that her secret lover's smile contorted with pain. But pain was not enough; fire must utterly destroy her.

I stood and watched as Karen's hair turned grey, then white, and her skin crumbled and withered. One eye still stared, defiant. Then that, too, winked horribly as it disappeared under an eyelid of ash.

I held the melting photograph until the flame seared my fingertips. I dropped the burning fragment. It fell on to the cardboard box. A moment later, the model aircraft pictured on the box seemed to lurch and try to take off. I watched as

166

fire crawled across the table among the scattered newspapers.

Then I turned like a sleepwalker and went slowly out of the house.

26

What the Hell Have I Done?

I stood on the hillside looking down at the back of the Midgley home. Through the uncurtained kitchen window I saw flames, like busy hands, working at the table. A glowing chunk of wood dropped on to the seat of one of four pine kitchen chairs and made itself comfortable on a bright blue cushion. It was like staring at something laid on as entertainment, nothing to do with me. I watched as all the chairs, then the beam above the Esse stove, and after that the window frame, joined the celebrating flames.

The glass in the kitchen window exploded. The noise broke through the trance-like detachment that gripped me. Karen's home was burning down; Karen and Jack's, who should have been my own son with Simon. My God, did I do that? What had I done?

I rushed back into the house. In the kitchen the fire already had a strong hold but I took a huge breath of the clearer air in the doorway and made a dive for the sink. The water from the taps hissed against the stone basin. I grabbed a saucepan from the draining board. I felt the handle brand the skin of my palm, but I scarcely noticed the pain. I hurled pan after pan of water at the flames doing their mad dance on the kitchen table.

The fire seemed to pause. In that moment, I saw a sight that transfixed me with horror. I saw the raddled painted face of Jean Midgley as she crouched against the doorway from the dining-room. Her eyes were fixed in a look of terror. She was not moving. Then she disappeared behind a bank of flame and smoke as fire caught the base of the grand-father clock.

I plunged across the room towards the cowering woman.

I couldn't see, the smoke was too dense. The clock collapsed as I made my way towards the doorway. It gave one strangled whirr like a young cockerel learning to crow, then disintegrated. I tripped against Jean Midgley and almost fell. I tried to pull her to her feet. She was a dead weight, unable to help herself.

I grabbed her under the arms and dragged her away from the smouldering wainscotting across the stone flags and out of the house. I dropped her on a patch of herbs, then crouched beside her, beating at her smouldering clothes with my bare hands.

I was gasping for breath. Each gulp of cold air was like a knife in my chest. I coughed and wheezed, retching as I tried to spit the foul smoke out of my lungs.

Jean Midgley was unconscious, but I couldn't make out if she was breathing. I didn't know how to tell or what to do. Desperately, I tried to remember something, anything, about first aid. Get air into the lungs, but how? My God, what the hell had I done?

And then I was pushed away, and there were people every-where. They didn't seem human, enormous and robotic in their fire-fighters' gear.

'She'll be all right now,' someone said, a strange sub-human voice through a breathing mask. 'Leave her to us.'

Who'd called the fire brigade? Who else was here? Who'd seen the fire?

Had anyone seen me, seen what I did?

I felt no connection with what was happening around me. There was nothing I could do. I watched the machine-like efficiency of the firemen. It was amazing that so many of them, lumbering in their protective gear, never got in each other's way. I couldn't look at the ambulance, where green-clad paramedics were working on Jean Midgley, trying to save her life. I caught a glimpse of the crisp grey frizz of singed hair among the hands and legs surrounding her. So much for bottled blondes, grey gets you one way or another. I fought down great bubbles of wild laughter which threatened to burst out of me, digging my nails into the palms of my hands to distract myself with the pain. It worked. It was agony. I'd forgotten that my hands were burned.

I was praying under my breath like a little child, Oh, my God, don't let her die. She can't die. I didn't mean to do it. It's not my fault.

But it was my fault. I had done it. A hand seemed to have grabbed a fistful of my insides and be wringing them out. I slipped to my knees, clutching myself.

A policewoman, suddenly squatting in front of me, asked, 'Are you all right? Hey, are you all right? What's your name? Can you tell me what happened?'

'Is she all right?' I asked.

It seemed to me that I was speaking in a normal voice, but I heard the harsh, hoarse whisper which was all I could manage.

The policewoman glanced at the group around Karen's mother.

'She's in good hands,' she said. 'She's alive.'

'Thank God for that,' I said. 'I thought she was dead.'

'Did you get her out of the house?' the policewoman asked.

'Yes, but I didn't realize there was anybody in the house. There was the fire, and then I saw her.'

The policewoman smiled and put a hand on my shoulder. She said, 'You saved her life. She wouldn't have had a chance if you hadn't got her out of there. It was an inferno.'

'Yes,' I said.

'Hey,' the policewoman called to the paramedics, 'we could do with some help here.'

The policewoman's voice seemed to come from a great distance. Vaguely, I was aware of a rank smell of wet ash. It was painful to breathe, and it was hard to keep my eyes open, they were so sore. I felt very tired, too tired to think at all. I started to weep, and once I'd started, I couldn't stop.

27

A Night-time Meeting

There were a few hours, then, when I lost track of what was happening to me. I felt like a parcel passed here and there by the milling teams of firemen, police and paramedics who'd suddenly appeared and taken over at Karen's house.

It was like looking through the wrong end of a telescope, making everything remote and unimportant. I was put in a police car and following the ambulance taking Jean Midgley to hospital I thought I remembered seeing Doreen's astonished face as the cavalcade flashed through the village. Then there was a succession of faces blurred into anonymity by that particular expression of detached concern which characterizes the caring professions on duty. Police officers asked questions about what happened. I seemed unable to understand them. I was put in a wheelchair and pushed from one place to another through long, silent and very hot corridors where all I was aware of was the swish of rubber soles on vinyl and the smell of disinfectant.

Then the fog in my brain suddenly cleared. I was sitting on a bed in a cubicle. A prison cell? A hospital, it must be, my hands were bandaged. Two policemen were talking to me.

One seemed to have been writing down what I'd said in a small black notebook.

He looked up and said, 'You were walking on the hillside and you saw the fire, is that right?'

'The kitchen was on fire,' I said. 'I saw the flames on the table.'

'And you forced your way in?' the other cop asked.

'No,' I said, 'the door was open. I'm sure the door was open.'

It hurt to speak; my throat felt raw.

'And you saw the woman lying there?' the policeman prompted.

I was about to ask him what had happened next. I seemed to have forgotten, if I'd ever known. Why did they keep asking me questions I couldn't answer? Then what he'd said suddenly became real.

'The woman who got burned?' I cried, trying to get to my feet. My harsh voice cracked. 'Is she here? Is she going to be all right?'

The policeman with the notebook was writing busily.

'She's in good hands,' he said. 'Lucky for her you were passing. A chance in a million that was, if you ask me. It's pretty isolated out there once the tourist season's over.'

His colleague nodded. 'She'd be a goner if it wasn't for what you did,' he said. 'You saved her life.'

'Can I see her?' I demanded.

Both policemen looked startled.

'I want to see her,' I said. 'I've got to tell her I'm sorry.'

I could hear the note of hysteria in my peculiar painful whisper.

'I don't think it's possible if you're not family,' one policeman said. 'And you've nothing to be sorry about, she'd be dead if you hadn't done what you did.'

He was trying to sound soothing.

173

A nurse came in.

She ignored the two policemen. 'That's enough for the moment,' she said to me. 'We're keeping you in overnight, just to be sure.' She glanced at the bandages on my hands. 'I'll give you something for the pain. You should try and get some sleep. You've done quite enough talking for today,' she said.

She pulled back the curtain for the cops to leave, showing disapproval by still not looking at them.

The nurse was about to follow them out, but I said, 'Can I see the woman from the fire? Just for a moment.'

'Not tonight,' she said. 'She's not up to visitors.'

'Is she going to be all right?'

The nurse hesitated. 'She's stable. Do you know her? I didn't know you knew her. She keeps muttering about someone called Simon – Simon and Karen. Have you any idea who they are?'

Those two names again, as casually joined as bread and butter.

'I don't know her,' I said.

'Oh, well,' said the nurse. 'Get some rest.'

She left, turning out the light.

I lay listening to the sort of hushed din of a hospital at night. I knew there was something tremendously important that I had to do, but I was still befuddled with the sedation. In a way, I was glad, because whatever it was that hung over me, it filled me with fear.

I tried to sleep, but every time I closed my eyes the walls around me seemed to turn to patterns of flame. I'd rather stay awake.

I tried to see the time, but my watch was gone. It seemed to be late at night. The nurses who passed the door talked in whispers and there was no sound of daytime hospital bustle.

I had to see Jean Midgley. I don't know why it seemed to

matter so much. There was no point in saying sorry now. It had been an accident, but there was no use trying to explain. I'd been so sure the house was empty, Karen out at Andy's cottage and Jack away with his schoolfriend. I'd forgotten Karen's mother. I hadn't even thought about her.

Hadn't John said she'd gone home with some old yokel? No, he hadn't said that exactly. It had been a guess. Anyway, I'd made enough noise looking round the house. Surely the woman couldn't help hearing me? Unless she'd drunk herself into a stupor after my stunt with the funeral flowers. She must have been drunk, and being drunk she wouldn't have felt much. That was what I told myself at least, as though it excused what I'd done, but of course it didn't.

Getting out of the hospital bed took more effort than I'd expected. My head kept spinning when I tried to stand. And breathing hurt like hell. But at last I opened the curtain and looked out into a corridor.

There was some sort of dim night-light burning in the main ward. I could see two nurses sitting at a desk. One was on the phone, the other reading a magazine. Both had their backs to me.

My room was on a short corridor leading to the open ward. Opposite I saw a door marked Sluice Room, and there were other offices and private rooms.

Jean Midgley was in a small room near the main entrance. The wall and door to the corridor were half-glazed. There seemed to be a spotlight shining on the bed where the woman lay motionless, attached by tubes to several machines surrounding her. I glanced back at the nurses who were presumably checking their monitors behind the desk in the ward.

I slipped into Jean Midgley's room.

Her hands were grasping at air on the stiff sheet. The bright red polish on her nails was badly chipped. She muttered, the fingers contorted. I wanted to flee. This was my fault; I'd created this horrible suffering creature on the bed and I wanted to run away and pretend it had nothing to do with me.

I stepped as close to the bed as I dared and took one of the restless hands.

Jean Midgley opened swollen, red-rimmed eyes. I caught a glimpse of bright, watery blue. But the woman simply stared, not seeing.

She muttered through blackened, cracked lips, 'Karen?'

She thought I was Karen. She wanted Karen. I hesitated, then tried to press her hand, but the bandages on my own hands ruined the gesture.

The pattern on a monitor beside the bed jerked and blurred. The nurses would see that at their station.

'I've got to go . . . Mum,' I said. My voice was a harsh growl.

'Don't you feel bad about Simon,' Jean Midgley suddenly said quite clearly, but I couldn't tell if it was a question or an order.

I asked, 'What do you mean? What are you trying to say?'

Jean stared at me, apparently unseeing. I pulled open the door and bumped into a nurse.

'What are you doing here?' the nurse asked.

'I'm looking for the loo,' I said.

'Well it's not in there,' the nurse said. 'You shouldn't be here.'

'I'm sorry,' I said. 'Where should I be?'

The nurse pointed, pushing me out of the way to get to Jean's side.

I returned to my room. There I sat on the edge of the bed, listening to a flurry of activity in the corridor.

I told myself that even Karen's own mother, even her drunken tart mother, thought Karen should feel guilty about what she did to Simon. Did I really think that, or was I trying to console myself and appease my guilt?

Or was Jean trying to comfort her daughter, telling her it wasn't her fault Simon was dead?

I repeated the words in my head again and again, hearing Jean Midgley's voice as she struggled to speak, a total lack of expression or emphasis as she pushed each syllable out.

Was she asking a question, admonishing Karen: 'Don't you feel bad about Simon?' Or reassuring her: 'Don't *you* feel bad', implying that she knew Karen had reason for feeling so.

What difference did it make now? Either way, I knew now that Jean knew what Karen had done. That made her an accomplice. She deserved to suffer too.

Of course I knew I was trying to find a way of easing my own guilt about the woman's injuries. She was Karen's mother, what else could a mother do? Jean didn't lie; she simply didn't tell what she knew about the truth. I told myself no mother would, specially when she'd blamed Simon for destroying Karen's life. Perhaps she didn't know that anyone else had been hurt by what Karen did. She didn't know about me.

I still couldn't sleep. At last I went to the desk in the ward and asked a male nurse for a sleeping pill. He seemed just to have come on duty. He glanced at a list on the desk and nodded. Then he gave me a pill with a beaker of water to help swallow it.

'Busy night?' I said, handing him back the empty beaker. 'Something seems to be going on.'

'Someone just died in one of the single rooms,' he said. 'I expect that's what you heard.'

'Who was it?' I asked. In spite of the hospital heat I felt very cold.

My voice was harsh and made the question sound peremptory and urgent.

The male nurse looked surprised. 'The woman who'd been in a house fire,' he said.

For him such a death was routine, but after glancing at my face he asked, 'Someone you knew?'

'No,' I said, 'I thought I'd saved her life.'

What I'd really done was kill her, I'd killed Karen Midgley's mother. I was a murderer.

28

Over Her Dead Body

The police asked me for a formal statement.

If they ask the question, I told myself, I'll confess everything.

But they didn't. No one asked if I'd started the fire in Karen's house and so killed Jean Midgley. No one even asked a leading question, like what was I doing there? It was extraordinary, but they had me down as the good guy and as far as they were concerned, I was way above suspicion; it never occurred to anyone I could've done such a thing. It wouldn't have occurred to me that I could, either, if I didn't know I had.

Everyone assumed there'd been a tragic accident. I even heard one of the policemen tell his senior officer that the dead woman had been an accident waiting to happen. There was only one possible conclusion to draw: Jean Midgley, drunk as usual, had stumbled downstairs to look for the bottle of whisky she'd left in the kitchen. There'd been a power cut. She'd tried to light the lamp. She'd knocked it over and couldn't react quickly enough to stop the fire catching hold. And everyone was so convinced of what had happened, I decided that even if I confessed everything, no one would believe me. But at least my conscience forced me to question the consensus.

'Are you sure it wasn't arson?' I said. And again, 'Why are you so sure it wasn't manslaughter?'

The police laughed at me. The nurses said I was suffering from reaction. Ask me, I pleaded silently with them, if you ask me I'll tell you the truth.

I said to a nurse who came to replace the bandages on my hands with a simple dressing, 'I could have done it. Don't they think it's odd that I was passing by? Why don't they think of that?' I felt guilty that even my burns weren't as bad as they'd seemed.

The nurse laughed. She told the policeman what I'd said. They both laughed.

'That's what comes of being a journalist,' the policeman said. 'Never let the boring truth stand in the way of a good story.'

The young constable who drove me back to Brockbeck had no doubts.

'A clear case of accidental death,' he said, and added, 'you could find yourself winning some kind of medal for what you did.'

'I didn't save her life,' I said. 'She died.'

The constable didn't say anything after that.

If they tell me it was an accident often enough, I thought, I'll come to believe it. Imagine getting a medal for what I did; whoever said God didn't have a sense of humour?

I stared out of the car window at the wind-bleached grasses and skeletal gorse scrub that stretched as far as the eye could see on either side of the long straight stretches of the road. The only vehicle we passed was an abandoned small digger tipped drunkenly into a ditch.

I told myself I hadn't meant to kill her, it *was* an accident, there was no point in stirring things up. Nothing was going to bring Jean Midgley back to life. But something had niggled at the back of my mind since I'd heard Jean was dead. I didn't want to formulate the thought, but it was there all the same. It was monstrous. I couldn't stop feeling that what I'd done was, if not exactly excused, at least mitigated by the favour I'd done Karen. She might not admit she'd wanted her mother gone, but she must have done. She was free now. And Jack would be better off not burdened by having a drunken tart as a grandmother. He might not realize now, but once he was a teenager it wouldn't be easy to live down having Jean as a granny.

Jesus, what kind of person was I? Jean Midgley was her mother, for God's sake. But it was no good telling myself that. I did feel that I'd released Karen from the shackles of a nightmare life, and it fuelled my resentment against her. It didn't occur to me even to question my own hold on sanity. It seemed logical to me. So far, all the harm I'd tried to do her had made things better for her. So far? That was really why I'd gone along with what people thought had happened to Jean. Deep inside, I knew I hadn't finished with Karen yet. She hadn't started to pay for killing Simon. Hadn't her own mother said so? They were her last words, meant for Karen – 'Don't you feel bad about Simon?' Or perhaps there wasn't a question mark at the end of Jean's sentence. I wasn't sure.

But it wasn't over, nowhere near it.

'She ain't seen nothing yet,' I said aloud.

'Did you say something?' the young constable asked.

'Who called the fire brigade?' I asked. 'That's what I'd like to know.'

I was still afraid that someone might have seen me at the farmhouse. The police could be playing cat and mouse with me.

'Oh, that was another stroke of luck,' the constable said,

'like you happening to walk by. There'd been a power cut reported. The electricity board was checking the power lines. The helicopter pilot saw the smoke and reported it.'

I said, 'Living up here must take some getting used to.' My voice was still a painful croak.

'Weirdos, if you ask me,' said the constable. 'Weirdos and sheep, that's what we used to say about the kids from the country when we were at school. I'm a town boy myself.' He laughed.

I thought of Jack. Did he suffer at school from town bullies who thought he was a weirdo? Poor Jack, once it would've been an advantage to be able to say you were Simon West's son, but now it must make things worse. Poor little Jack. I'd make it up to him one day, when all this was over. He'd thank me for it one day.

'Here we are,' the constable said, driving up to the door of The Black Bull.

John, like mine host in a Dickens' story, came out to meet us.

'Anything to carry?' he asked, opening the door to help me out of the car. He smiled at my hands as though they confirmed something he'd been challenged on.

'Not even a handbag,' I said, 'but thanks.'

John looked startled at the sound of my burnt-out voice. He didn't understand what I'd said.

'Come in and have a drink,' he said.

The constable didn't get out of the car. 'You're in good hands, then,' he said. 'I'll be getting back.'

John seemed about to take my elbow to help me inside, but he thought better of it.

'What a thing,' he said. 'Poor old Jean.'

I whispered, 'You'll miss her.'

'We'll miss her,' John said, 'But you're a heroine all the same. You did all you could,' he added.

In spite of his sorrowful tone, he couldn't hide his excitement at the great event of the tragic fire.

'What a thing,' he said again, 'a fire like that. Jean Midgley dead and Karen and the boy homeless. It don't bear thinking of.'

The bar was unusually busy for the time of day. The villagers' information was built on snippets of gossip and speculation. All they knew for certain was that Jean Midgley had died in a fire at the farmhouse. But no one stopped at that. They crowded at the bar and asked each other if Karen was safe, where Karen was, had Jack been at the house? The one thing they didn't speculate about was what had caused the fire. No one even questioned that drunken Jean must have started it herself.

So before I could stop him John presented me to the people at the bar as though I was a local horse who'd won the Grand National. Doreen, too, stopped serving and ran to greet me.

'Oh, hinny, thank God you're restored to life.'

It was as though I'd been turned into a different person as far as she was concerned, like someone getting a knighthood.

Doreen went on, 'We've heard the brave thing you did, rushing into that raging inferno without a thought for yourself to save poor Jean, God rest her.'

They crowded round me, as though being close to me could bring them luck.

I didn't know what to say or do. If I told them now that I'd started the fire, they wouldn't believe me. Or they'd lynch me. There'd been a tragedy in the community and what they needed was a gallant, albeit unsuccessful, heroine to counteract the tragedy of Jean's death. They wouldn't thank me for telling them the truth.

It was scary. I stood blank-faced as they milled around me, and all I could think of was Simon. This was what it had been like for him all the time, these crowding, clawing people baying at him like this. I was terrified. He had loved it though. It made him feel wanted. But surely he must have felt unworthy of their adulation, knowing that he was not what they believed him to be? For me that was so terrifying that I clung to the lie.

No, Simon hadn't felt like that, he'd never doubted himself, not as long as they loved him. It was only when they withdrew their love after his arrest that he got frightened, face to face with the fact that he was alone. He was done for after that. He'd had no inner resources whatsoever. He was always a child, undeveloped as a real person.

I was suddenly overwhelmed by bleak despair at the prospect of all the empty future days without him, mere child as he was.

I managed to mutter, 'It was nothing. Anyone would've done the same.'

My raw croak gave them pause. They pressed closer, trying to make out what I'd said, demanding answers.

'What happened?'

'Where did the fire start?'

'What did you feel?'

The pressing questions were a refuge. They gave me no opportunity to answer any of them.

One voice said, 'They say Karen knew nowt about it till Andy Little brought her home next day and found the house burned down.'

'Yes,' another said, 'she thought Jean was at the pub. Next thing she knows, her ma's dead and gone.'

'The police were trying to find her for hours. They should've asked us where she'd be. How would they know about her and Andy Little?'

'That poor girl, and the wee boy.'

I recognized Betty Carter's voice, though I couldn't see her among the crowd. It was brave of her, countering the crowd's mood.

'The house is a write-off,' Daniel Carter said. 'What's she going to do?'

'The insurance'll pay,' someone said.

There was a general snort of derision. 'What bloody insurance? How'd they afford insurance?'

'She'll move in with Andy Little,' Betty Carter said. 'They'll get married sooner than planned, that's all.'

'They've got all the flowers they'll need for the funeral, anyway,' Doreen said. 'That'll save a few bob.'

No one laughed at this bad-taste joke but someone said, 'Andy Little wouldn't have been looking forward to having Jean Midgley live with him after he and Karen got wed.'

'You don't think. . . ?'

'You're not saying. . . ?'

This was getting out of hand. I could stop it, I had to stop it. I put up my hand. They all fell silent as a bank of eyes like television cameras swivelled to stare at me.

I struggled to get words out, my throat straining.

'No, no one started the fire like that. Jean started it. It was an accident. She knocked the lamp over in the power cut. That's what the police told me.'

'Yes, Jean would've been drunk,' someone said. 'She was always drunk.'

They were satisfied. It was the obvious explanation. It had been bound to happen sometime, the way she drank.

But later, alone in my bedroom, I felt ashamed. It wouldn't have been right to let the rumour-mongers hound Andy Little with their innuendoes. But what I'd done was just as unfair, letting the dead woman take the blame because it couldn't hurt her now.

I was as bad as the people who thought when Simon killed himself that it confirmed he was a rapist. But I wasn't as bad as Karen. Those stupid people who'd hounded Simon to death and then after it didn't know what they were doing; nor did I when I caused Jean's death. But Karen was different. She'd known exactly what she was doing when she destroyed Simon.

I wasn't going to let her marry Andy Little and live happily ever after. Over my dead body.

I shivered as I remembered poor Jean Midgley saying those same words.

And I thought, Jean's dead, hers were empty words. But mine aren't.

29

My One Reason for Living

Someone was playing an accordion. I lay in bed with my
hands throbbing and tried to ignore the noise. It was long
after dark and the crowd who'd been in the bar for hours had
begun to sing the old traditional sentimental songs. Then
someone with a strong voice started on 'The Old Rugged
Cross'. It was a comic version of the hymn, I could hear
people laughing. I thought of the Methodist chapel across
the road standing impassive in the face of such mockery of
old-time religion and I wondered if it wasn't inviting bad
luck.

There was a knock at my bedroom door. I took no notice.
But someone opened the door and came into the room.
Beyond the range of my bedside light, it was too dark for me
really to make out who it was, but I knew at once that it was
Karen. I jumped to my feet.

'You?' I muttered, hearing my voice still weak from the
fire.

Karen didn't understand my feeble croak. 'I'm Karen
Midgley, you gave me a lift in your car once,' she said. 'It was
my mother you tried to save from the fire.'

187

It was weird, realizing that someone I felt I knew so well, the object of my intense hatred, was until now almost unaware of my existence. For her I was merely a kind passing motorist.

She came closer to the bed, into the light.

She looked tired and pale, her eyes red-rimmed.

But she was still beautiful, and I wondered, would I hate her so much if she weren't so good-looking?

'I came to thank you,' Karen said. 'What you did was incredibly brave.'

I stared at her without speaking. I couldn't speak.

Then I managed to say, 'How's Jack?'

Karen looked surprised. 'You know Jack?'

I shook my head. 'I don't know Jack. John downstairs mentioned him, that's all.'

'Oh.' Karen sat on the edge of the bed. She kept picking at the coverlet, pleating and unpleating it with long, thin fingers. She had bitten, dirty nails. She said, 'You must think I'm terrible, leaving my mother alone like that. I thought she'd be in the pub all day. She usually spends most of the day there. She did, I mean.'

'None of my business,' I said. I hadn't noticed before, but Karen had a slight local accent. I hadn't expected that. It didn't seem fair that someone as good-looking as she was should have a lovely, distinctive voice like that.

Karen said, 'Jack's away this week and Andy, my boyfriend, and I get very little chance to be alone together. I stayed over at his. I know it looks bad, and if I'd known . . .'

'It wasn't your fault,' I said. 'You shouldn't blame yourself.' My voice broke and my throat throbbed.

Another chorus of 'The Old Rugged Cross' almost made the pictures on the wall shudder. Many discordant voices had now joined in with the original singer.

Karen smiled. 'I should leave you to get some rest,' she

said. 'I should've left it till the morning to come, but I had to thank you.'

I put out my hand to stop her going. Karen turned back and leaned forward.

'Got to talk,' I croaked.

'Any time,' Karen said. 'Of course. I'd be grateful. I need to know what happened.'

Suddenly I thought I had to have it out with her. I needed to know what had happened to make her do what she did to Simon.

'Tomorrow,' I said.

The words came out like a cough, but Karen appeared to understand. She put out her hand as though to touch my arm, then withdrew it.

'Thank you again,' Karen said. 'You're a real heroine. I wish there was something I could do to show you how I feel about what you did.'

'Anyone would've done the same,' I said.

Karen had scarcely left when there was a pounding at my door.

I ignored it, hoping whoever it was would go away.

More banging, then a man's voice.

'Sara, let me in. I've got to talk to you.'

'Who is it?' My voice was almost completely gone now.

'I know you're in there. Do you want me to break the door down?'

I opened the door a crack. In the light from the corridor, I saw the greedy drunken pig's face of Ted, the *Gazette* reporter.

'Ted!' I said. 'What are you doing here?'

For a moment, all I could remember about this bouncy, overweight little man was that he was the reporter who'd covered Simon's original court hearing and, later, his trial. Why was he here? What had he come to tell me about Simon now?

He pushed past me into the room.

'For God's sake, what kept you? I've paid off the man behind the bar to keep quiet, but the place is teeming with the opposition.'

I was still confused. 'What's up?' I asked.

He turned on the overhead light and sat down on the bed as though the room was his.

'Why didn't you ring the office? I can tell you, Frank took a pretty dim view when he heard what you did, and not a peep out of you.'

I was blinded by the light. And bewildered.

'What are you on about?'

'Come on, Sara, get a grip. Are you on dope or something? You drag a woman out of a blazing house, risking life and limb in a heroic rescue bid, and you're surprised to see me here? What kind of reporter are you?'

'I'm not a reporter, I'm a sub.'

I was angry with myself. Of course I knew what I should have done. Once – before Simon died – it would have been second nature to ring Frank. But it was different now. My career at the newspaper seemed like an abandoned day-dream.

I made an effort to pull myself together, though. I could see that Ted was suspicious. I wasn't acting naturally at all, and he was impatient.

'It's the drugs they gave me in the hospital,' I said, trying to placate him. I didn't want him to start asking too many questions about how the fire started, that kind of thing. 'I got burned, and inhaled smoke, so they gave me something that makes me confused. Sorry, Ted.'

He seemed only now to notice my bandaged hands. He tried to look sympathetic, but he was in a hurry.

'OK,' he said, 'but I need a few quotes. I've got the bones of the story from the people in the bar. It's the chief topic of conversation. But I need something from you. You know that woman died?'

'Yes.'

'How do you feel about that?'

'All that trouble for nothing, you mean?'

Ted looked relieved; this was more like the Sara he knew. He started to write in his notebook.

'Hey,' I said, 'that's not a quote.'

'No,' he said, 'We've got to give the readers what they want, and that's not your cheap cynicism. I'm just saying something suitable. Heroic rescue attempt, tragic ending, that's what I'm after. Did you know the woman?'

'She drank here in the bar.'

'I know that! Landlord's best customer; regulars' best friend, always prepared to sit down and listen to a tale of woe; prop and stay of inadequate single-mum daughter and innocent grandson. I've got all I need of that sort of thing. What I need from you is House of Hell, choking smoke, the heat of the flames beating you back, bursting lungs, the smell, the kid's smoke-blackened toys — you know the drill. And then finding out the old biddy had died in spite of it all, your sense of guilt . . .'

'*Guilt*? Why should I feel guilty?'

'OK, OK, of course not guilt. Not in that sense. But our readers like their heroines to feel a bit guilty about their heroics being unsuccessful. You know the sort of thing – if only I'd done this or not done something – that makes you seem more human.'

'I think that just about covers it,' I said. 'You could've been there!'

Ted didn't get irony.

'Right,' he said. 'Now all I need's a picture of the wounded heroine.'

'No,' I said, 'you won't make tonight's last edition with a

picture anyway. You'd be better off trying to talk to the daughter. You must've passed her on the stairs.'

Tom looked horrified.

'My God,' he said, 'was that the daughter? If she goes in the bar, Dave Petley from the *Star* will get hold of her.'

He rushed out of the room and I heard the pounding of his feet on the stairs.

I was certain that Karen wouldn't have gone into the bar. Andy Little was probably outside in his pickup waiting to take her home with him. Ted would be searching the village for hours looking for a quote from her.

Once he was gone, I became aware of the silence. There was no sound now from the bar downstairs, no traffic noise from the street. I lay on my back staring into the darkness. I was suddenly homesick for Castleborough, with the friendly noise of other people all around me. The silence here was positively threatening, implacable.

I was frightened, really scared of the future. Ted's coming had brought it home, he'd barged in to remind me of the real life I'd left behind, empty without Simon. Somehow, without even noticing, I'd cast myself adrift since I'd been in Brockbeck, lost control of who and what I was, and what I was doing. This wasn't what I'd wanted. Everything was out of control and I didn't understand what was going on. None of this was going to help avenge Simon. And nothing whatsoever was going to bring him back. I'd done a dreadful thing and I'd gained nothing. Until then I'd sort of assumed that if I could punish Karen and make her pay, I'd go back to Castleford and find everything miraculously the same, with Simon on the phone asking where the hell I thought I'd been and what I'd been doing there.

But that wasn't going to happen. I couldn't kid myself any more. I closed my eyes and tried to see Simon's face. I thought of the floppy fair hair, the beautiful symmetry of the bones of cheeks and jaw; the way his mouth curled a little when he smiled; the dark-blue eyes that had been the first thing I'd noticed about him. He'd always been able to turn my knees to jelly with those eyes of his. I remembered how that had felt; I recalled each separate feature, but I couldn't recapture his face as a whole. What scared me most of all was the fear that I wouldn't recognize him now if I saw him. Hatred for Karen, jealousy because of Jack, the urge to hurt the person who had hurt Simon, all these were more real now than the man himself, or even what had happened to him. And I'd changed; I'd become a monster. A monster who still wasn't satisfied that Karen had paid for what she'd done. The one reason I had for living was still the compulsion to destroy her life.

30

Chinese Whispers

That night I couldn't sleep. My hands still throbbed a bit, and my chest hurt, but it wasn't that.

Without taking any conscious decision, I knew what I had to do. After that, there would be an end to this nightmare.

I got up early and went downstairs. Ted was in the bar, sitting slumped on a stool staring at a pint of flat beer. He was alone and he looked a sick pig.

'You look terrible,' I said.

'People in glass houses . . .' he said gloomily.

'Did you find Karen last night?'

'Who?'

'Karen Midgley.'

He shook his head.

'She didn't come in here. Dave and the other boys from the nationals were here, so I couldn't ask about her. You've only just missed them. They've gone to look for breakfast. We were here all night. Landlord left us to it.'

He yawned and stretched.

'What's the time?' he asked.

'Time you got moving. Didn't you hear what I said?'

'What about?'

'Karen Midgley. Midgley, for God's sake. Simon West?'

'What's Simon West got to do with it?'

'Oh, Ted, get a grip. Karen Midgley was the woman in the Simon West case.'

Ted turned to look at me. 'What are you on about? Honestly, Sara, you've lost the plot.'

I wanted to shake him, the stupid, drunken slob.

I said, 'Don't you understand? That woman who died in the fire, the one I tried to save, was Karen Midgley's mother.'

He still looked blank and I spelled it out for him as to an inattentive child. 'Karen Midgley made up the rape allegations against Simon West which drove him to kill himself. The dead woman was Jean Midgley, Karen's mother. Good story, yes?'

I saw the familiar transformation take place. Gone was the obtuseness after a night's drinking. He was alert, wide-awake, geared for action.

'Jean Midgley?' he cried, 'It was *that* Jean Midgley!'

He gripped me and gave me a smacking kiss on the mouth.

'My God,' he said, 'I nearly missed it. The way you kept going on about the daughter nearly put me off the scent.'

'I know where you can find her,' I said. 'Karen, I mean.'

'Later, babe, later. If she's anything like her mother, I'll pass on her. That woman nearly castrated me once. Jean Midgley, the pitchfork gladiator. I must put this over for the *Evening News* and then get on to the TV people for the lunchtime bulletins. Can you believe it: the woman who accused Simon West of raping her, burns herself alive? I'll see you right, too, kid, there'll be a tip-off fee in it for you.'

I didn't even hear what he was saying. I simply stared at him. He seemed suddenly almost to disappear, and his voice came from a long way away. I grabbed the edge of the bar to stop myself falling.

'What are you on about?' I said, in the hoarse whisper which was all I could manage. 'You told me it was Karen Midgley who accused Simon.'

'I've never even heard of Karen Midgley,' Ted said, putting down the empty glass. 'I never told you that. Thanks for jogging the old memory, though. I owe you one.'

He hurried away. He hadn't noticed the shock on my face. He'd scarcely heard what I'd said.

My God, he'd said Karen Midgley, he must've done. Otherwise why would I think it was her?

But then I thought, No, he'd said Midgley. That was all. And then when I asked Simon if he knew someone called Midgley, he'd said he knew Karen. Or was it Marta Blane who first mentioned Karen?

'Jesus,' I said, 'what have I done?'

31

An Early Morning Visit

It was getting light. The sky above the dark shadow of the hill was a clear green, but the new moon still showed above the roofs of the village street. I walked quickly past the sleeping houses towards the track that led to the burnt-out farmhouse.

I killed that woman, I kept repeating to myself, I killed her, and I kept trying to tell myself that she deserved to die. Jean Midgley had driven Simon to his death. All I'd done was to take revenge. It was fate. I'd punished Simon's persecutor without realizing what I was doing. A life for a life; one unintentional death for another.

But it didn't help, I couldn't justify what I had done, even to myself. And, what was worse, I knew I wouldn't have felt like this if it had been Karen who'd died. I'd be glad, then. If I'd killed Karen, I'd be happy, even if she hadn't ruined Simon. I hated her, not Simon's accuser.

No, that couldn't be true. Karen was innocent, and she was the mother of Simon's child, I'd no reason to want her dead. Except that Simon had loved her and she was pretty and sexy and vibrant with life and I was none of those things.

I pressed my fingers hard against my temples, trying to re-adjust my brain. It was grotesque that Jean Midgley had made the allegations against Simon. It made a nonsense of everything. It made Simon absurd that he had killed himself because of that raddled old whore. No one could take her seriously. Anyone could see that she was mad. How could the police have believed her? They probably didn't; they'd liked the idea of humiliating someone rich and famous like Simon. They'd have loved the chance to present that human wreck as evidence against Simon. And once they'd started the ball rolling, all those freaky little wannabe victims had come forward to claim their moment of glory and the cops were only too happy to be involved in a front-page case against a celebrity.

And then I thought, Jean Midgley wasn't always like that. Before Karen came crawling home with her baby and her tales of Jack's glamorous television-star father, she hadn't been a sexually frustrated drunk. But why would she suddenly accuse Simon? Did she want attention? Or was Karen to blame after all? Had Karen told her mother things that made Jean want revenge on the man she thought had ruined her daughter's life? But why should she wait so long to take it? I could only think that Simon had always been in contact with Karen, that he'd told her about me, said he had a new love. If Karen had told Jean that, it might have triggered that demented mother's malice.

My chest was on fire climbing the hill. The cold air hurt my scorched lungs. I moved slowly, glad of the pain as a distraction from my thoughts. But it wasn't enough.

Why did it make so much difference that it was Jean and not Karen? It being Jack's grandmother made the whole thing into a sick joke, but it was more than that. If it had been Karen . . . did I really think Simon might've been guilty if it was Karen? Was that why I hated her so much, because I hadn't trusted *him*?

I tramped on.

I had to see Karen. I didn't know what I was going to say when I found her, but I had to see her.

I didn't hate her any less, I'd done a terrible thing to punish her for something she didn't do, and yet I still hated her. That wasn't right, it wasn't sane.

I asked myself, Am I going to tell her what her mother did?

Would she believe me if I did tell her? She had been Simon's girl. She'd had his baby. Had she known what her mother did? Perhaps she'd known all along.

I could have gone to Andy Little's cottage. But I had to see Karen alone. There were animals at the farm. Sooner or later she must come to feed them. Fire or no fire, the animals had to be looked after.

When she came, I'd be waiting, she wouldn't get away from me this time.

When I reached the farm and looked back the way I'd come, the hillside looked like a sheet of glass in the rising sun. The stiff grass and heather were shrouded in dew-drenched spiders' webs which caught the rays of the sun and sparkled like expensive jewellery. My own footprints showed black, like a vandal's paint. Wisps of thin grey mist curled round the boulders above me on the track. It was magical, so beautiful that I stopped for a few moments to gaze at it.

But then the house loomed out of the haze.

Without glass, the windows gaped like eye sockets in an ancient skull. Otherwise, from the front, there was little sign of the fire damage. It was at the back that the stone wall was scarred black, the kitchen door and all the window frames charred and destroyed. The place smelled foul.

Karen Midgley was standing in the ruin of the kitchen.

'My God,' I said.

I was aghast. I'd done this, caused this hideous destruction. I remembered the way this room had been, the comfortable armchair, the towering old panel clock, the pots and pans now reduced to unrecognizable twisted metal. And the colours, the rag rugs, the child's bright pictures on the white walls, the bold chintz flowers on the upholstered chair, all reduced to ashy black. Even the cream-coloured Esse stove was now a dull dark grey. Out of spite, I'd destroyed Karen's home, her refuge. And Jack's. There was Jack, Simon's son, and I'd done this in spite of knowing that I was destroying his world. This was the only home Jack had ever known. I felt horribly ashamed.

'I'm so sorry,' I said.

Karen looked at me and shrugged.

'I didn't expect you to come here. I was going to come to the pub later.'

'I had to see the damage,' I said. It hadn't been my reason for coming, but it was now. I'd had to come to see what I'd done.

'This is the worst bit,' Karen said. 'The rest of the house isn't so bad.' She hesitated, carefully not looking at me.

'Where was Mum?' she asked at last.

I pointed at the doorway into the interior of the house.

'She'd come through that door,' I said.

I'd thought my voice had recovered, but I heard how thin and weak it sounded.

'Inside that door,' I said again.

'You were very brave; you must've gone right through the fire,' Karen said, and I was once again aware of how attractive her voice was. 'I can't imagine how it must have been,' Karen added, 'everything burning and you having to drag her all that way through the flames.'

'I'm so sorry,' I said again. Her attitude made me feel ashamed, yet I still wanted to hurt her.

'I know,' Karen said. 'Poor Mum. I only hope she didn't know too much about it.'

'I saw her in the hospital,' I said.

'I wish I'd been there.'

'There's no point in thinking like that,' I said.

'I can't get it out of my mind,' Karen said.

She moved stiffly like an automaton out of the ruined kitchen. I followed her into the almost empty dining room I'd seen through the window when I first came to the house. The heavy dark table and the four chairs I'd seen then were undamaged.

Karen opened the door of a cupboard built into the wall. She took out two glasses and a bottle of whisky.

'Mum never found this,' she said. She smiled.

She poured whisky into the glasses and pushed one across the table to me.

'I hope you don't mind me asking questions,' she said. 'I don't want to make you go through it all again if it's too much, but it would help me a lot to know . . . you know, not being there in time. Was she in much pain?'

'No,' I said. 'I don't think she was really conscious. They'd given her something. She was confused. She thought I was you. It seemed kinder to let her think so, and I did.'

'I'm glad,' Karen said. 'At least she didn't know she was alone.'

'She said something to me, thinking I was you.'

I hesitated, looking for the right words. Karen waited, leaning across the table towards me. What did she expect, some sentimental death-bed declaration of love? I almost wished I could've given her that, but I couldn't go back now.

I took a deep breath and said, 'Your mother said, "Don't you feel bad about Simon".'

32

Just Good Friends

Karen looked puzzled. 'What an odd thing for her to say,' she said. 'What did she mean? Was that all?'

'That was it. Don't you even know who she meant?'

I could feel my burned hands start to thump with pain under the bandages. My knees felt weak, and I was glad I was sitting down.

Karen said, 'She must've meant Simon West. I didn't tell you because I didn't want to talk about it, but he was an old friend of mine.'

'*That* Simon West?' I could scarcely say Simon's name.

'I knew him long before he was *that* Simon West. He was working with a television producer called Mike. I was madly in love with Mike. He was the first man I ever lived with. The only man I ever lived with.' Karen gave a rueful little smile. 'Then I had to tell him I was pregnant and he dumped me. Mike did, not Simon. Mike said it must be someone else's, but it wasn't, he was the only man I'd ever slept with. I was devastated. Simon was a good friend to me; he let me stay at his place.'

I stared at Karen. I ought to stop her, I thought, I should

tell her the truth now. But I couldn't. I had to know about
her and Simon.

Karen said, 'Simon saved my life, he really did. I don't
know what I might've done. I didn't know what to do. I was
so naïve; you wouldn't believe how naïve I was. I'd been
working at the TV station as a freelance. Mike was my boss.
When he dumped me, I couldn't go on working there. We'd
lived in his house, me and him. I had no job, no money,
nowhere to go, nothing. And the baby on the way. Simon was
a real friend.'

I managed to ask, 'But why did your mother say you
shouldn't feel bad about him? Why should you feel bad?'

Karen shook her head. 'Because he's dead, I suppose.'

She paused, obviously remembering something suddenly.
Then she smiled and said, 'I actually did him a big favour. He
said so, anyway.'

I fought down waves of sickness. I was sweating, but I felt
icy cold. 'Yes?' I whispered.

Karen laughed. 'I suppose there's no harm now. Poor
Simon.' She broke off, then started again. 'Have you heard of
Marta Blane? She made it big in America for a while. But
before that she was mad on Simon. I've never seen anything
like it. She couldn't see it was just a fling for him. She was
desperate to marry him. She wouldn't leave him alone, she
was always following him around and bombarding him with
marriage proposals. It was really embarrassing. She wouldn't
take no for an answer. So Simon and I cooked up this plan
that he and I were an item.'

'Did it put her off?'

'Well, I was pregnant. I don't know if he actually told her
it was his baby, but that's what she would have thought. Yes,
she went to America and the rest is history. . . .'

'So you and Simon never . . . were never really lovers?'

'No, of course not.' Karen looked as though she thought

203

the question astonishing, but then her face cleared. 'Oh, you've heard the stories in the village, have you? After all this time, you'd think there'd be some fresher gossip they could get their teeth into.'

'Yes,' I said, 'I'm sorry. I heard your son's father was a TV celebrity, so when someone said you'd known Simon West, I thought the child must be his. And then when you told me you didn't know him, I thought you'd got something to hide and that was it.'

Using Simon's full name sounded odd to me, spoken here between his lover and his friend, but it made it easier for me to speak about him without revealing my emotional turmoil.

'No,' Karen said, 'Mike was Jack's father, whatever that means. He's some father. He's never even seen him. But Simon came to visit once or twice, I suppose people jumped to conclusions. I know Mum did. At the time, I didn't give a damn what people thought. And thinking it was Simon stopped Mum pestering me about who it really was. Mike was married, you see. He'd got kids. He was scared, I guess there wasn't much he could do, but at the time . . . I was only seventeen. It doesn't seem important now I've got Andy. I told Andy about Mike the other night, and he wanted to track him down and beat him up. It took me some time to get him to drop that stupid male kneejerk stuff, but still I felt better once I'd told him.'

I had to look down. I couldn't meet that clear blue gaze. I wanted to say that I knew she'd told Andy something important, that I was sitting at the next table in the bar eavesdropping, but I was sure she was talking about Simon, not Mike.

Karen paused, then smiled at me. 'I never talked to Mum about things like that. I just couldn't, although she was always trying to make me. Could you, with your mother?'

'God, no,' I said. I shuddered at the thought, much as my

mother had shuddered at the subject of sex. 'I believed I'd been left under a gooseberry bush till I was practically grown up because that was the only way I could see my mother getting a baby.'

'Funny how two extremes can have the same result,' Karen said. 'Mine had so much sex with so many men I grew up thinking it was a kind of household chore, like Hoovering the floor. I didn't want any of it. Then I fell in love with Mike, and it seemed to have nothing to do with what my mother was always talking about.'

'I'm so sorry,' I said.

Karen was plainly surprised at the depth of real feeling in my tone then. She gave me a quick look with her clear blue eyes, then turned away as if embarrassed.

'You're sorry about a lot of things, aren't you?' she said. 'Don't be. You've helped me a lot. Now I think I'll be able to come to terms with what's happened. You told me what she said, and although I don't understand what she meant, I needed to know.'

She got up and put the bottle of whisky back in its cupboard.

'Silly,' she said, 'I don't have to hide the whisky any more. Not that it was really hidden from her; she must've found it after all. It had been watered, hadn't it? Good old Mum.'

'I was going to marry Simon,' I blurted out. 'We were going to be married. I was in love with him. We were in love.'

Karen turned to look at me. Without saying anything, she brought the bottle, watered or not, back to the table, poured both of us another drink, and sat down again.

'You and Simon. . . ?'

'We kept it secret. He thought it would be bad for his career if he had a regular girlfriend.'

It sounded absurd, even to me. Spoken aloud like that, it was surely obvious that I was laying claim to something that could never have been real.

'That's how it was,' I said, defensive.

Karen smiled. 'That's so typical of Simon,' she said. She spoke softly. 'It must've been awful for you, what happened.'

She put out her hand. I recoiled.

'Please, don't be nice to me,' I said. 'I've got to finish this.'

Karen didn't look surprised. She sat back and waited.

At last I pulled myself together. I took a deep breath and blurted out, 'I thought you were the one who accused him of rape.'

Karen was nonplussed. 'You what? You thought I made up a story that Simon raped me?'

She looked at me in amazement. Then she started to laugh. 'My God,' she said, 'what gave you that idea? You must be crazy. Or else you need help.'

'I know. I think I do.'

Karen stopped smiling. She refilled my glass, then her own.

'Simon and I were never even lovers,' she said. 'We never would've been, even if I wasn't in love with Mike. Simon never felt anything like that for me.'

'I know. I know that now. But one of the reporters at work said something and I was in such a state I put two and two together and it just went on from there. . . .'

'You'd better tell me.'

I had to tell her, I had to tell her that it was her mother who accused Simon. She had to be told.

'Ted – the reporter – was in court for Simon's case and mentioned someone called Midgley,' I found myself saying. 'I suppose it came up about what happened with Marta Blane.'

Why had I said that? I knew that wasn't what happened.

'I thought . . .' I said. 'I asked Simon if he knew anyone with that name. He said he knew a Karen Midgley. And then I came here and saw Jack and I thought . . .'

I'd never wanted so much to run away and disappear. But it was too late, I'd got to tell her now.

But I said nothing.

Karen was looking at me as though she and I were from a different species. Her voice, though, was gentle, as though she were being careful talking to someone insane in case she sent them off the rails.

'But you thought Simon was Jack's father. You really thought I'd accuse my son's father of rape? How could you think that?

'I saw how you lived. I thought you'd made it up for money. If Simon wouldn't pay, the papers would.'

I broke off because I couldn't control my voice.

Then I sobbed, 'I was jealous. I thought he'd loved you and that Jack was his son. I wanted his baby and he wouldn't and then he was dead.'

Painful tears racked my burning throat and chest.

Tell her, I told myself, before she reads the whole sorry story in the paper.

But still I couldn't do it. I couldn't say the words.

Karen watched me. She looked inscrutable. Then she pulled a wad of tissues from her pocket and pushed them towards me.

'It's all right,' she said. 'I think I even understand.'

'There's more,' I said.

'No,' Karen said. 'Not now. Please, that's enough now.'

'I need to tell you.'

'I've got to feed the calves. And I need to be alone for a bit. Can't you see, it's too much to take in. I don't want to know any more. I don't even know you.'

'Please, Karen.'

'No, no, no,' Karen said, pushing me away as she ran out of the room.

33

A High Price for Revenge

In The Black Bull, John was reading a newspaper behind the bar. Two old men, the regulars, were playing dominoes. It seemed as though nothing had changed since that first day I'd walked in there, looking for Karen. Yet so much had happened. I felt a completely different person from the woman I'd been then.

John took one look at me and poured me a dry white wine without being asked. With a landlord's tact, he didn't comment on my tear-stained face.

'The circus has moved on then,' I said.

He leaned across to put the glass in front of me. He looked terrible, too. I shuddered, remembering a few long nights of my own in bars in the company of the representatives of the press.

'Feels like a morgue after all that excitement,' he said. 'Your friend left a message for you.'

'Ted? I hope he didn't tell you I'd pay his bar bill?'

'No, nothing like that.' John looked puzzled. He wasn't used to the ways of journalists. 'No, he said to tell you to enjoy your fifteen minutes. And he said to make sure you read this.'

He folded the newspaper he'd been reading and pushed it across the bar so I could read it without having to use my bandaged hands.

I saw the picture of Karen's blackened farmhouse set in a stark grey landscape that might have illustrated a Gothic novel.

'Oh, God,' I said, 'what kind of nonsense has he written?'

'You should be pleased enough,' John said. 'You're all right, it calls you a heroine. But there's a lot of stuff about Jean being a drunk and a tart and how round here we all thought she was a bit of a weirdo, which isn't right, it isn't right at all.'

John looked upset. There was sweat on his bald head. I knew there was more in the newspaper story, but he was too embarrassed to tell me.

So I asked, 'What else does he say?'

'It's what it says there about Karen, making out she's some kind of wild tart who left her helpless drunken mother and the boy to go out at night to meet lovers. It quotes that advertisement for her services in the local paper. That's not fair. One thing about this tragedy's for sure, it wasn't Karen's fault, and it's not fair.'

More lies, more perceived truth, I thought, damn Ted and his silly emotive clichés.

'It's as well for him he's gone,' I said. 'This is rubbish,' I added, pointing a bandaged hand at the newspaper.

'I told him so when he came to pay his bill,' John said. 'He said it's only what the public wants to hear. Do you think that's really true?' John shook his head and turned the newspaper so he could look at the picture again. He added, 'That may be true among those fellows, but it don't seem right to me.'

'It isn't right. Or true,' I said.

'Couldn't you write a letter to the editor saying it isn't?' John said.

We were both silent for a while. I could tell that he took it for granted that a protest would help to put the record straight. I didn't know how to explain that no forms of denial would alter the facts as they had appeared, however false. Everyone in the village could write letters repudiating the story, and the newspaper could even print them, but I knew that there was no changing the readers' belief in what they'd already seen in print.

'Best ignore it,' I said, 'that's the quickest way it'll go away. Karen's friends know it's rubbish.'

So, I thought, the lie wins out again. The truth has no way of fighting back.

John looked doubtful. One of the old men called for another round. 'I've got to change the barrel,' John said. He disappeared down the stairs to the cellar.

I stared at the headlines. This was yesterday's news; it would be worse tomorrow when they read that Jean was the woman Simon West had raped. *Allegedly* raped, the sub-editor in me corrected, but I knew better. No one believed in Simon's innocence. I'd given Ted the story myself, but I knew only too well that when Ted's follow-up came out, the world would brand Simon a freak as well as a rapist. Raping a young woman like Karen was one thing, a horrible crime, but raping a grotesque superannuated bleached blonde tart like Jean Midgley was something else. It was perversion. It was also ludicrous. Simon had been a sex symbol. What kind of sex symbol raped a woman old enough to be his mother?

I was a bloody fool to remind Ted about the Simon West case. Without my prompting, he might just not have made the connection. I did it out of spite, to make Karen suffer more. And she was innocent, as innocent as Simon.

What I'd done was make her pay for her mother's crime, and I'd made Simon pay for my revenge.

Other people had paid a high price for that revenge, too. There was Jack. I'd destroyed that child's home and killed his grandmother, and he had nothing to do with it at all.

The worst of it was that while I thought Simon was Jack's father, I'd really believed I was justified in what I'd done to avenge him. As long as Karen was the enemy, I'd taken on myself some kind of responsibility to look after Jack by defending Simon. I'd been prepared to love the boy because he was all that remained to me of Simon. Yes, I'd loved Jack. I hadn't gone so far as to plan a future for the two of us, me and him, without Karen, but it had been in my mind that that was what would happen.

But that was crazy and the boy wasn't Simon's son. As the child of Karen and the elusive Mike, he meant nothing to me. But my new emotional distance from the boy made me more guilty then ever over what I'd done to harm him.

I didn't know what I could do to make amends. But I couldn't leave things as they were. It wasn't over yet.

34

Goodbye to Brockbeck

I was sitting on a boulder, staring at the sky. Mountainous ranges of cloud looming behind the summit of the hills created a savage and precipitous continent behind the near horizon. The sky seemed vast. In the city, in Castleborough, it always appeared reduced, bounded by man-made buildings; here I could believe it was infinite and powerful. This place was beautiful, and I'd never even noticed.

But it was awe inspiring, not real. At least, this place, and the people in it, had never seemed real to me and yet what I had done here was horribly real.

Oh, God, I'd been such a fool. I'd thought Castleborough and the newspaper and the crowded city was reality, but there we were just going through the motions of mass cohabitation. It was out here where reality counted, where people had to face the truth about themselves if they were going to survive. But I couldn't face the truth. I wanted to go home and escape all this and go on pretending like all the rest. I was running away from reality.

My bill was paid at the pub, my bags packed and stowed

in the car. I should have been well on my way south by now.

It was no good, though, I couldn't leave it like this. There'd been too much lying and it was all destructive.

I'd been drawn back here to the burned-out farmhouse whether I liked it or not. The last thing I wanted was to force Karen to listen to me, but I must. I kept faltering, staring at that vast sky and telling myself I should simply flee. I tried to tell myself that Ted's story about Jean Midgley would be a brief sensation, then quickly forgotten. Let it go. As Frank, who loved a cliché, would have said, 'Least said, soonest mended.'

No one would ever know I was a murderer. No one doubted that poor, confused, drunken Jean caused the fire that killed her. She was dead; my lie couldn't hurt her. Simon was dead. Nobody remembered he'd known Karen. It would be so easy to go away and leave things as they were. Easy for Karen, too; she wouldn't have to face the truth.

There was nothing to stop me. And no one could blame me, after all. What had happened wasn't my responsibility. Other people's lies had caused all this. Silly lies that didn't seem to matter at the time. Simon had lied to his fans about himself to create the image he wanted. Well, if he hadn't actually lied, he'd withheld the truth, at least about his relationship with me. I'd colluded in that lie, that was all.

Karen had lied about Simon, too. She'd let her mother believe that Simon was Jack's father. It'd been the easy way out. Ted, too, had deceived me when he'd said Simon's accuser was called Midgley without saying it was Jean, not Karen, Midgley. Maybe he hadn't realized what he was doing, but he'd held back on the truth.

God, I told myself as I thought all this, how unfair I was. I couldn't believe I was saying these things, even to myself.

Jean Midgley had lied, too, deliberately, and she hadn't been able to stop her lie until it was too late. Even if she'd tried, the lie had already become the public perception of the truth. So Simon had died. I told myself that perhaps, if his life hadn't been based on lies, he might have been believed when he told the truth. But that was wishful thinking. Truth or lies, people believed what they wanted to believe, it didn't matter.

Why make it worse? I asked myself.

I took one last look at the huge monumental sky.

What did it matter in the scheme of things what I or anyone else had done?

I thought I'd decided to keep silent. I was sure I had made up my mind to walk back to The Black Bull to collect the car and drive away from Brockbeck, leave the place and all the people in it behind for ever.

But when I got up to go, I began to walk slowly up the hill to the ruined farmhouse.

I'd got to put a stop to the lying. If no one tried to tell the truth because it was easier not to, really there was no point in going on. It was bad enough facing life without Simon, but at least what we'd had together was real and good even if it was hidden behind the lie.

That was a lie, too; I was lying to myself. What Simon and I'd had together wasn't real and good, it hadn't been for some time. There was no point in being sentimental now. I did what I'd done because I couldn't admit that everything had changed. Simon had loved me, I believed he had, but he wasn't capable of a real love relationship. And my love for him had been found wanting, too. I'd sometimes dreaded our future together in the weeks before his death.

I was responsible for what had happened since then, and I'd got to take that responsibility; I couldn't live the rest of my life feeling ashamed to be me.

I almost turned back when I reached the house, though. But instead I walked in.

Karen was in the ruins of the kitchen. She had made a start on clearing out the blackened stumps of furniture and the twisted metal that had once been her pots and pans. I could hear her swearing to herself as she tried to dislodge the wreckage of shelves and cupboards. I could see where she'd tried to wash the fire stains from the flagstone floor; those areas now looked dirtier than the untouched slabs, streaked in wet soot and ash like camouflage canvas.

Karen jumped when I came in. Her hair looked as though it had been used to scrub the fire-scarred walls. Her face was black, streaked grey where she'd tried to rub away the tears that poured down her cheeks and neck. Her red-rimmed eyes were the only flash of colour in the monochrome scene.

I wished Simon could see her, he wouldn't think her so bloody beautiful now. But he hadn't thought her beautiful, that was only what I'd imagined. And when I looked more closely and saw that underneath the grime Karen's beauty still shone through, I felt sick.

'Oh, it's you again,' she said. 'What do you want this time?'

'You must hear me out. I've got to talk to you,' I said.

'I've told you I don't want to know. You've got a hell of a nerve, coming here, even if you did try to save Mum.'

'Karen, it's about your mum. And me. And you, as well. I've got to warn you.'

Karen looked hostile, but she said nothing.

I said, 'I want you to know that if I could go back and do things differently, I would, but I can't. When I've told you, you'll have to do what you think's right. If you go to the police, I'll take what's coming.'

'The police?' Karen said. 'What do the police have to do with anything?'

'I started the fire. I killed your mother.'

Karen stared at me. She didn't believe what she'd heard.

215

'What kind of person are you?' she cried. 'Do you think this is some kind of joke?'

I ignored her. I went on as though I was reading from a script.

'I told you I thought you'd accused Simon. I believed it. I wanted revenge. That's why I came here. I wanted to hurt you. There was a photo of you and Simon . . .'

'You did that? You came in my house?'

'I wanted to destroy everything between you and Simon. I burned a picture of you, I left it burning.'

'My God,' Karen said.

'I came back when I saw what I'd done. I didn't know your mother was there. I tried to save her.'

'My God,' Karen said again.

She turned and went through the blackened gap where the door to the rest of the house had been. I followed her.

In the dining-room, the bottle of watered whisky and our two glasses still stood on the table. Karen sat down heavily and poured herself a drink. Then she poured one for me.

I searched for what to say next, but Karen interrupted. 'The reporter said Midgley, didn't he?' she said. 'That's why you thought it was me. You said so, didn't you?'

This was disconcerting. Karen's question seemed to have nothing to do with what we were talking about. I nodded.

'So it was my mother? Is that what you're trying to say? My mother accused Simon? Is that why you killed her?'

'No,' I said, 'no.'

I tried to meet Karen's eyes but I couldn't.

'Yes,' I said, 'it was her, she accused Simon. But I didn't know that. The reporter who came here after the fire told me. He knew it was her, but I didn't know until she was already dead.'

Karen put her hands over her face. Then, after some time,

she dropped them to the table. When she spoke, her voice sounded flat.

'I want to call you a liar,' she said, 'a crazy liar. But you're not lying, are you?'

'It's going to be in the papers,' I said. 'That's what I wanted to tell you.'

There was a brief silence. I stared at my hands clenched in my lap.

Then Karen topped up her glass and laughed. I couldn't believe she laughed.

'Poor old Mum', she said. 'She always wanted to be somebody famous in the papers.'

I said, 'I'm so sorry. I didn't mean to hurt her.'

'There's not much point in all that now,' Karen said. 'Your sorry's not a lot of use, is it, even to you? You may not've meant to kill her, but she's dead.' Her voice trembled as she fought back tears. 'I don't suppose Mum meant to hurt Simon, not really, but she did. And he's dead, too.'

We neither of us spoke for a while, then Karen said, 'It's partly my fault. I suppose I knew she thought Simon was Jack's father. It was easier than telling her the truth. I never gave it a thought. Mum must've held it against him all these years. And then he came here once when she was drunk and I was out and she hit on him. She'd do that with anyone. Simon ran a mile. He told me why. That was the end. He stopped coming. I suppose she never forgave him for humiliating her. And I was angry with her because she'd driven him away and Jack loved him.'

'But why did she wait all this time to accuse him?'

Karen shook her head. 'It was probably an accident. He was a star. She was probably stringing a line to some guy in a bar about the old days and got carried away. She was always reinventing the past. She believed the stuff she made up when she was drunk.' Karen hesitated, then added, 'She wouldn't mean it to go as far as it did. She must've been amazed when the cops took it seriously, but she'd have liked the attention. She was probably drunk when they interviewed her. When they believed her, she probably forgot she'd made it up, by then she probably thought it was true anyway.'

'But surely she knew how you'd feel?'

'She may've thought she could frighten him into coming back into my life. She always thought that was what I wanted, and I think she knew she'd driven him away from me. She'd never liked the idea of me and Andy. She thought I loved Simon because he was famous and successful and because Andy isn't like that, he wasn't right for me, not in her eyes.'

'That's why she didn't like Andy?'

'She never really knew him. Not as a person.'

'But you love him.'

'Yes, I really love him. But Mum wouldn't understand that. She never loved anyone in the whole of her life, not even me. And I was always ashamed of her; I feel bad about that now. Ages ago, she came to Leeds when I was working there to ask me for money and I wouldn't meet her.'

Karen paused, trying to stop her lip trembling. She took a deep breath and went on, 'The last thing I wanted was for Mike to meet her. I was terrified of losing him. You know, I even hoped then that once Jack was born I'd have him adopted and Mike and me could be together again as if nothing had happened.'

She smiled the smile of a loving mother who can't believe she could ever have been so deluded.

Could I ever think like that? Could I ever have been prepared to give away my child because the man I loved didn't want to be a father and it was the only way he'd stay with me?

I tried to tell myself I couldn't ever have done such a thing, but I knew in my heart that I could and I would. I'd have done it for Simon. If I'd got pregnant and he didn't want it, I'd have done anything as long as he'd stay with me.

I looked at Karen and Karen was looking at me. I turned away quickly, embarrassed because I knew that Karen guessed what I was thinking. She'd got over Mike however much she loved him, she'd put all that behind her and she'd made a life for herself. I'd loved Simon like that, I still did, but I didn't know how to do what she'd done. She pitied me for that.

Karen went on, 'And she was afraid Andy and I would leave her here alone. Yes, I suppose that's what it was all about. She was afraid to be left alone. But it wasn't going to be like that.'

Karen ran her hand through her hair, then added, 'That's one of the things I love about Andy. Mum was horrible to him. He couldn't stand her, either. But it never occurred to him she wouldn't come to live with us. It was me didn't want that.'

'I didn't want to kill anyone,' I said. 'I wanted you dead, but I don't think it was ever real. I think it was a way of dealing with what happened to Simon.'

Was that true, I wondered, was there no more than that to all those hours of plotting to have her dead? Something between a computer game and a storyline in a TV soap?

'You must've really hated me.' Karen sounded as though she found this curious. 'Do you still?'

'Hate you? How could I? I wanted to hurt you because of Simon. I thought you'd driven him to kill himself. I hated you for that.'

I hesitated, then added in a voice so low Karen had to lean across the table to hear me, 'I can't help it. It doesn't just disappear. I need someone to blame because I feel everything's over for me, but no, I don't hate you. I suppose I was jealous of you.'

219

Karen didn't ask why I was jealous, she seemed to take it for granted. Instead she said, 'God, it's so stupid.'

'Stupid?' I asked.

'You hating me, and then finding out I didn't do it. Did it ever occur to you that it was your fault Simon killed himself? Face it, it was you he didn't want to stay alive for.'

There was a long silence.

Karen and I stared at each other in horror. We were like two climbers united in terror on either side of the crevasse that had suddenly opened up to swallow our mutual friend. Each of us was very aware of the sound of the other's heavy breathing. There was nothing to say.

Outside the window a startled blackbird cried a warning. It was getting dark. At last Karen leaned forward to pick up the whisky bottle.

'One more?' she said. She poured the whisky into the glasses.

I was about to say something. Karen put up a hand to stop me speaking.

'There's nothing to say,' Karen said. 'Leave it at that.'

'What do you want me to do? I'll go to the police if you want.'

Karen got up. 'What's the point? It won't change anything. Think how it would be for Jack if everything was raked up again. I don't think you'll be getting off easy. If anything, I feel sorry for you, having to live with what you've done. I wouldn't want to be you.'

'*I* don't want to be me.'

We walked through the rank smelling kitchen and out on to the hillside.

In the open air, it was still possible to make out the outlines of the house and farm buildings, and the fold of the hill against the sky, but it was nearly dark. Millions of stars already studded the vast expanse of sky, shaming the cluster

220

of lights from the village below in the valley. But the lights in the village looked more friendly.

We walked down to the village together in silence.

Outside The Black Bull, we stopped.

'I'll pay for the house,' I said. 'I saved money to marry Simon. I'll give it to you.'

'I don't want your money,' Karen said. 'Jack and I will move to Andy's place. I'll sell it as a conversion project to some rich yuppy in television, or something like that. I never want to go back to that farmhouse now.'

'I must do something,' I said. 'Please, at least let me do something. I could put money in trust for Jack.'

'Jack's nothing to do with you. We don't want anything from you. Leave it at that. Mum's dead. What people think won't hurt her now. And she did cause Simon's death. I don't have to make you pay for what you did. I reckon we're even, Sara Soames.'

The use of my full name was like a blow. I felt my eyes burn with unshed tears.

'Do you think we could've been friends?' I asked, in a voice so low I wasn't sure Karen heard me. I added, even more faintly, 'We both loved Simon.'

'Yes,' Karen said, 'we did.'

'So, friends?'

'No,' Karen said. 'I'm going to meet Andy and we'll get married when Jack comes home and we'll be a family. You've nothing to do with us, so get out of our lives and don't come back.'

'Do you think you'll ever be able to forgive me?'

'I think I may find it easier than you will. I hope you can build yourself some sort of life.'

She walked away down the street. There were a few lights in windows above the shop and post office, but no other signs of life.

221

I called after her. 'Goodbye. Good luck.'

There was no reply. Karen had disappeared into the shadows.

I walked to my car and drove slowly away from Brockbeck towards Alderdale. There were no lights I could see in Andy Little's cottage as I passed, no sign of human habitation at all, just a dark wood beside a lonely road.

In Alderdale, I saw the first road sign mentioning Castleborough, with Leeds, Sheffield, and other cities to the south. I was on my way home.

Already Brockbeck and what had happened there seemed unreal, just as the nightmare last weeks with Simon now seemed to have happened during some sort of trancelike time-out in my life. At some future stage, I knew, I'd have to confront those unsuspected demons in myself which had turned me from a normal, perfectly ordinary young woman into someone I didn't even recognize as me. Till then, though, I was fleeing to my life in Castleborough, to the regulated security of the city where generations of ordinary people like me had created an ordered system of living far removed from places like Brockbeck where, it seemed to me, people struggled as best they could for physical and emotional survival against chaos. I'd learned there that even I, a contentedly unremarkable woman, could, and did, revert to instinctive savagery when driven to protect my illusions of reality.

Back in Castleborough, back to my home, my job, to Frank, even, I would have the chance to rebuild the normal, ordinary life I wanted to live. I knew it wouldn't be easy. I thought I might start by asking Fortuny why she didn't change her stupid name. She and I might even be friends if she had a normal, ordinary name.